CONFESSION

First published by Charco Press 2023
Charco Press Ltd., Office 59, 44-46 Morningside Road, Edinburgh
EH10 4BF

Copyright © Martín Kohan 2020
First published in Spanish as *Confesión* (Anagrama, 2020)
English translation copyright © Daniel Hahn, 2023

Work published with funding from the 'Sur' Translation Support
Programme of the Ministry of Foreign Affairs of Argentina / Obra
editada en el marco del Programa 'Sur' de Apoyo a las Traducciones del
Ministerio de Relaciones Exteriores de la República Argentina.

A CIP catalogue record for this book is available
from the British Library.

ISBN: 9781913867652
e-book: 9781913867669

www.charcopress.com

Edited by Fionn Petch
Cover designed by Pablo Font
Typeset by Laura Jones
Proofread by Fiona Mackintosh

Martín Kohan

CONFESSION

Translated
by Daniel Hahn

CHARCO PRESS

Note to the reader

The third part of this novel, beginning on page 121, describes a conversation that takes place over a game of cards. The game being played is truco, a trick-taking game that is very widely known in Argentina, but which you're unlikely to play if you're reading this in the Anglo world. It is perfectly possible to read the section without knowing how the game works (I did). But if you would like to prepare yourself, you'll find the basic rules of truco explained by Michel Nieva in an appendix on page 163.

Daniel Hahn

For Alexandra

I

MERCEDES

Father, I have sinned. I've sinned, or I think I have, said, and says, Mirta López, my grandmother. Who wasn't my grandmother yet, of course: she was only twelve. Kneeling in the confessional at the church of San Patricio, over in Mercedes, aware of Father Suñé, who was leaning forward, just like her, towards the porous wooden grille, in the comingled smell of incense and the damp of the floor and walls, in the thick gloom from the stained-glass windows that are too high up and probably dirty, as she awaited the double promise of understanding and punishment, of acceptance and rebuke, of indulgence and sanction, presenting tolerance with something maybe intolerable, approaching forgiveness with something perhaps unforgivable, Mirta López, my grandmother, the girl who would much later be my grandmother, white blouse and blue skirt and an elastic headband, also blue, holding and ordering her hair, said this: I have sinned, and then: or I think I have. The verbs conjugated in that way, the present perfect, an appropriate form for confession and for all solemn pronouncements (for promises, the future: I won't do it again; for sins, the present perfect: I have lied). She said and says, in those exact words, and although when speaking today she raises her head, for a better evocation, at the time she lowered it, ashamed: chin touching her chest, her eyes lost on her own hands, a contained sob.

There was a silence. It's not only sounds that echo, silences echo too; that happens in churches, and it happened in the San Patricio one, over in Mercedes, after my grandmother Mirta spoke. In that silence, which was troubling, it did occur to her that her words, the way she

3

had murmured them, were less like a confession than a question. Then, from the other side, she heard Father Suñé's voice:

'You have sinned? Or you think that you have sinned?'

The verbs conjugated in the present perfect, and, besides, using the familiar *tú*.

Indeed: what she had formulated, the way she'd formulated it, was really a doubt and not a confession, or at least not a confession just yet. Which is why that invisible priest, the voice of Father Suñé, from that kind of sacred hidey-hole called a confessional, was unable to utter, he could not, either penance nor absolution, but could merely do what in fact he did: return the doubt to her, ask for more clarity.

'You think you've sinned? Or you have?'

Mirta López didn't know. Or rather, she wasn't sure. That good existed, on the one hand, and that evil existed, on the other, oh, she was perfectly well aware of that: she learned it at communion, she had sensed it earlier and she'd recently had it ratified when she got confirmed in the Mercedes cathedral. God and Lucifer, heaven and hell, virtue and sins; simple as that. Well, then? So why could she not answer? Father Suñé was waiting. The church of San Patricio was waiting. She felt herself being assailed by dizziness and tears. She rested a hand on the wood, the better to support herself, and firmly planted the twelve years of her knees intact on the barely padded covering that received the guilty. Lying is always a sin; here, in God's house, it's a mortal one. But she was not going to lie, of course; she didn't know, that was the truth. Better, then, to tell what had happened, what it was that had happened to her, and let it be for Father Suñé, with that smell of damp and incense that might have been his and not the church's, finally to establish, discerningly, whether she had sinned or not. And if she had, then what sin it was. And with what penalty she would redeem herself.

So my grandmother spoke. She had confessed throughout her childhood: a lie to her schoolmistress in first grade, yanking Cecilia Pardo's plaits in second, the theft of an eraser in third, a bad word said in fourth. That sort of thing. Now, however, having completed primary school, having been through her Confirmation, she had the unerring impression that she was confessing for the first time in her life. She wasn't going to forget this day – 6 March, 1941 – for that reason. Then Mirta López said, she said to Father Suñé, that sometimes she felt a powerful tremor, a kind of whirlpool, only hot, in her stomach, in her whole belly, a thing kind of like a fever and a perspiration, a sudden feeling of alarm and bewilderment, and that it was only by bringing her legs together, no, not bringing but squeezing them together, and not her legs but her thighs, that it was only then, yes, squeezing her thighs together, that she managed gradually to calm herself, gradually to restore her tranquillity.

There was a pause and there was a silence, which wasn't, not remotely, the same silence as before. Father Suñé cleared his throat.

'Where do you feel all that, exactly?' he enquired.

'Here,' said my grandmother, and she pointed to herself; but the gesture meant nothing. She, too, was invisible now, at least to Father Suñé. She would have to describe it. So she did: 'That's it, like a whirlpool. It goes up or down, and it spins round me. Here, in my stomach.'

'Your stomach, ah yes,' Father Suñé confirmed this. 'But your legs, what about them?'

'My legs come together, they squeeze together,' replied Mirta, my grandmother; 'or I've got to squeeze them together, Father, it's the only thing that calms me down. It becomes like a kind of a bubbling. Then I'm all calm again.'

Father Suñé fell silent. She could just barely make him out, back there, thinking.

'And do you touch yourself?' he asked as last.

Mirta didn't understand at first, she wondered if she'd heard him right. She said something, she can't remember it now, a babbling, only half-words. The priest seemed to suspect that she was being evasive. He raised his voice. There in the church.

'Your hands, girl, your hands. What do you do with your hands? Do you touch yourself?'

Mirta thought about a piano, about candy, about boiling water: those things you were and were not allowed to touch. And she said no: she didn't touch herself.

Perhaps the priest nodded, in there: agreeing or relieved.

'Do you have wicked thoughts?' he went on. His voice sounded gentler: 'When all this happens, do you have wicked thoughts? Abominable pictures in your mind?'

Mirta, my grandmother, she now says, sobbed. And that was a confession to herself, before it was one to Father Suñé, to his voice, to his questions; before it was one to Our Lord God, who is all-knowing, who is all-seeing. Because she, of course, was not lying, you don't lie in confession, it's the same as condemning yourself to hell. But she was, yes, keeping things quiet, omitting things. And the sin of omission, well, it's in the name, is still a sin.

She didn't find the San Patricio church as scary as the cathedral, which was bigger, though less dark. But she did still find it scary. And Father Suñé's voice wasn't unfamiliar to her, she could recognise it right away, and while it inspired confidence in her, it inspired fear, too. She wouldn't have been able to tell him what at that moment she did tell him if she could have seen him: face to face, his dark eyes, his eyebrows, his frown. But that was just it: she could not. She could not have seen him even if she had looked; and she didn't look.

Mirta López then said that she did not have wicked thoughts, absolutely not. The whirlpool, the alarm, the fever and the stifling, she had provoked none of it herself, by imagining this or that. The desire to squeeze her thighs together: that, she said, she says, didn't result from any fantasising either. But nor did it just happen of its own accord, at any old moment, or just because. It happened whenever she saw – through the window of the dining room of her house, on the opposite pavement, or worse still, that is to say, better still, on the near pavement – the Videlas' eldest son going by.

'He isn't their eldest son,' Father Suñé corrected her. 'There were two other sons born before him.'

'But they're dead!' exclaimed my grandmother, her voice too loud, and she was startled to hear it bounce off parts of the church: the altar, the pulpit, a poor-box, the crucified Christ. She reverted to a whisper: 'they died a year later, poor little angels. Of measles.'

'I know,' the priest persisted. 'But they do exist. They died but they exist in the Kingdom of God. Baptised by me, just as you were: Jorge and Rafael.'

My grandmother didn't contradict him, but she reasoned: that in leaving when still so tiny, without even having grown, she'd always seen the next son, who even carried their names, as the eldest. The fact is that, en route to the railway station, because he was studying in Buenos Aires, or returning from the station, for that same reason, he always walked right by her house. Sometimes closer to the window, if he was on the near pavement, sometimes a tiny bit further away, if he was on the opposite one; but he did go past, always. Upright and serene. And she, on seeing him, would hurry to the window, concealed behind the net curtain, to get a closer view of his passing and so that that passing would last longer. And it was then, just then, on reaching the armchair, or actually a little earlier, from the very moment she saw him, that the hot whirlpool began, it would climb up her belly, it would climb up and also down, a heat as if from lack of sleep or from having eaten too much, a kind of fever and breathlessness in her temples and in her chest, and all this at once sank into her, or overflowed, and she'd get that urge to squeeze her legs together like she'd already told him about, that urge or that urgency to bring her thighs together and squeeze, seeing the Videlas' eldest son moving away towards the corner, his steps firm and the back of his neck so fair, drawing the curtain a little and looking out but no longer afraid of being seen, the evening, the pavement, the trees and the big Mercedes sky.

So said and says Mirta López, my grandmother. And she says that Father Suñé remained silent for a bit, maybe half a minute or less, but which to her seemed a whole century. Until at last he spoke and asked: if she'd had any wicked thoughts. Not before, nor during, but afterwards. Mirta López said she hadn't. To which Father Suñé asked: if she'd had wicked dreams, sinful dreams, after that. Mirta López said she never remembered what she dreamt, she didn't have that ability, but that her teacher in fifth grade, Miss Posadas, had told her that we all dream dreams; that dreaming always happens; only she didn't remember having had bad dreams afterwards, and if she'd had them she was sure she would have remembered, and no, she didn't remember any, so no: there had been no bad ones.

She heard the wood creak in there, the other side of the confessional. Father Suñé had moved.

'You are free from sin,' he concluded.

Mirta López gave a sigh of relief.

'Childish over-excitement, that's all,' the priest explained.

Mirta López, she can't say why, thanked him: twice, three times.

'You are free from sin,' said Father Suñé. 'Go with God.'

Father Suñé would have remained there a little while longer, in his little booth for listening and judging. He would have stayed unmoving, in the dark, as if waiting for someone else who might show up to clear out any regrets, tribulations. He would have heard, if not really noticed, the effect of the wooden heels on the church's chilly paving slabs, the steps with which Mirta López crossed the nave and moved away. He would then have heard the groan of farewell from one of the two swing doors: the girl had gone. He would have brought his hands together, and linked his fingers, as if about to pray, but without praying. He would have been left there thinking – about what? About God, presumably. Finally, after a time, he would have readied himself to leave the confessional. It is easier to be there than it is to go in (get inside and settle himself there) or come out (turn around and emerge), which was why he would have felt visibly agitated as he arranged his cassock with both hands, like somebody trying to get rid of wrinkles (but no, his attire would have looked impeccable) or looking for something in his pockets (but no, he mostly wouldn't use those pockets). He would have walked, then, through his church, slowly and dragging his feet a little: the friction of worn soles on a mundane floor. On passing the altar, he would have come to a stop, he would have bowed his head, he would have crossed himself; all gestures that seemed automatic, which he would have composed, however, in order to provide premeditation and hence to act knowingly. Then he would have disappeared, on the far side of the building, through one of those side doors that from the place of the faithful cannot be seen and which suggest, for that very reason, because it's not known where exactly they are nor where exactly they lead, that there are mysteries in the world of man, just as there are in the Kingdom of God, and that they too, albeit quite differently, are unfathomable.

Mirta López emerged from the San Patricio church with something more than relief: with gladness. She walked quickly down the clear pavement, but she could have run, or she could have done it, as she used to, while jumping rope. On this first block she didn't bump into anybody, but if she had, she would have greeted them or would have smiled at them, out of sheer happiness. She walked to the town's main square, the place with the most sun and the most light of anywhere. Until not long ago she had gone there to play with her girlfriends, the setting for her childhood, for her evenings and her summers. Now she turned, looked around her, sat down on one of the stone benches. She heard herself breathe. She was happy. There were no obstacles: she could go on spying through the window of the dining room of her house, on Saturday afternoons, on his return from boarding school in Buenos Aires, and on Sundays just before night fell, when he came back, the Videlas' eldest son, who'd walk past without registering her, supposing her, imagining her.

They say that the city turns its back on the river. And quite right. The reproach, which is spoken frequently, assumes something wasted, it suggests some neglect, some folly. The city has its river, as so many cities do: Paris and London and Frankfurt, or, rather nearer, Montevideo; the city has its best landscape there, the way Rosario has its islands or Santiago its mountain range. And yet instead of looking, it chooses to ignore it. Metaphorically or literally: it turns its back on it.

Is it wrong to do so? The river is horrible. It's thick and cloudy, it's dull and flat. It neither flows by nor does it offer anything; its swell, when the wind is blowing, is a mere imitation of the real thing, the frustration of a swell. It's worse than a motionless river: it's a river that doesn't even know how to move. It shudders, irregularly, or stalls on the spot, with neither rhythm nor grace, like an animal that's too big or a bulk too clumsy.

Where does it come from? From the Paraná and the Uruguay. But it has since lost all its virtues. Because you don't just see rivers flowing, you know they flow; that they are changing always, that they only stay while going; you're aware of the idea that they put into Heraclitus's head, and, with him, thanks to him, into everyone else's. And where does it go? Towards the Argentine Sea, towards the ocean. But it doesn't, any longer, have its qualities. Because you don't just not see the seas ending, you know they don't end. That's why they become horizon: because they do, indeed, arrive at the horizon. It's short-sightedness, that's all: a lack of angle, of perspective. With enough height (the height does exist, it's not just conjecture: there are rich people familiar with it on the upper floors of Avenida del Libertador), you can know that it does end right there, just opposite, over in Colonia.

A mess of mud and assorted grime, a bitter gathering of camalotes (if the wind blows from the north) or sinister onslaught of flooding and drizzle (if the wind blows from the south), the river is the city's nuisance. And when it isn't, because it sometimes isn't, it is still the possibility of a nuisance. It's good for getting to the city and for leaving; being on it, or beside it, or facing it, is harder, less usual. The business of fishermen, no more than that. And the fishermen are there, as still as the river, as glum as the river, just seeing what they can get out of it, just seeing if they can get anything out of it at all.

If the city were a house (which, of course, it isn't), the river would not be its front garden, its façade, its reception area. Nor, so to speak, its park. It would be what it is: its backyard. Its store of old junk, the last bastion of the discarded. The bit no one looks at. The bit nobody notices. The bit on which you must turn your back. Or also – and why not? – the back. Its actual back.

From all this there emerged a sort of deliberateness, a thing wrought of intentions and calculation, which in turn produced guilt: the conscience experiencing regret. Without this burden, my grandmother Mirta would not have felt the need to return to confession again so quickly. The occasional look from the window, though preceded by a certain watchfulness, or even, where possible, by a certain attentiveness, could finally be assimilated into the rhythm of daily life, nothing out-of-keeping with the habits of the home. With the same apparent inertia with which someone might move from the dining room to the kitchen, or stop in the entrance hall to briefly rearrange a vase, or sit down grumbling in the main armchair to read the newspaper, so she would go to the window, would look out, would focus on the street, would examine the pavements.

When she took to making inquiries, it was not a letting go. She knew that a great distance away (a hundred kilometres, at age twelve, feels like a great distance, and kilometres in those days weren't what they are today) was the big city. She had been to Buenos Aires, a few times, with her parents; but she hadn't liked it: she'd been stunned and saddened by how much there was of it, and the jumble. She learned, because she snooped around, that in a neighbourhood called Once, which exists in convention though not on the land registry's official plans, is that college, San José, in the charge of the Bayonne Fathers; and she learned that this order was more permissive than others, at least in some aspects (one example: they allowed smoking). The college, in that neighbourhood, couldn't be very far from a square, the Plaza Miserere, from a mausoleum, that of Bernardino Rivadavia, and hence from the big railway station. There the trains arrived, the ones from the west, which, if she wanted, she could watch leaving Mercedes. They would not look the same in one place as in the other: incredibly modern and incongruent in the lowly scatterings of the town, they would become, amid the clamour of the height and hurry, just one more element of so many.

The Videlas' eldest son (the first two, the twins, had died; as far as she was concerned, they didn't count), having passed sixth grade at Mercedes School No.7 (an act of devotion to his studies that the town remarked upon appreciatively), entered San José as a boarder. Being a boarder meant he slept there every night (she learned this from reading a book: *Juvenilia* by Miguel Cané), with those other classmates who had families in the provinces. Mirta López took great pains to imagine those nights, those shared rooms with their perfectly aligned beds, the combined breathings once the Bayonne priests called lights out; she wondered whether these specula-tions, explored down to the last detail, constituted what Father Suñé called wicked thoughts – perhaps she ought to mention them so that he might resolve this.

The boarders in those schools would leave on the weekends, unless their families lived at too great a distance: in Córdoba or Catamarca or Río Negro. That wasn't the case with Mercedes nor with the Videlas' eldest son. He would leave on Saturday, early, and walk, with a few others, to the station; there he'd take the train, the Sarmiento line. The train ploughed through streets, then neighbourhoods, then suburbs, then towns, then fields, before finally arriving in Mercedes. A shed, a big barn of a place, a couple of platforms, a lot of exposure to the elements: that was what the town's railway station consisted of. There he would arrive on Saturdays and from there he would return on Sundays. Those days were generally so quiet that my grandmother, from her house, in the silence of her room, could feel the rumble of the locomotive. A mixture of snoring and clattering that she experienced as happiness (because it was).

Nonetheless, she did want to add, to these signs, a greater precision. My grandmother Mirta set about memorising the timetables: arrivals and departures, durations and waiting times. The English trains, being English, were to all people the very parameter of regularity. Thus she could know, with almost no slippage, when the Videlas' eldest son would pass in front of her house; when on Saturday and when on Sunday; because it was clear that he kept not only the times, but also the route from his house (his family's) and the railway station, invariable, with the constancy of something pre-decided. Mirta López waited for him. More than nervous: with eagerness, with longing, about which nobody (apart from Father Suñé) had any idea or knew the score. Now seeing him was not only seeing him, the indescribable thrill of seeing him, but also of waiting for him. It wouldn't last more than the minute, minute and a half, that the event occupied each time, from his appearing, firm and serious, on one side, until he walked away and disappeared from view, on the other, always with just the same disposition. Now all of this began for her a little earlier, with the prelude, with the imminence; and in an effect of irradiation, of contagion or of symmetry, the time would extend a little afterwards, when everything had passed, when the Videlas' eldest had passed, and she however remained trembling, unsettled, half-entranced, feverish. What would have happened if at that moment, at any of those moments, she had been surprised by her mother (my great-grandmother) or her father (my great-grandfather)? What excuse would she have offered? What explanation would she have given?

My grandmother doesn't know. She doesn't know, can't imagine. Fortunately, she says, it never happened. And that's just it, that's what the experience consisted of, that's just what it was: the world around her ceased or faded, as happens to theatre audiences when the show is about to begin, or to those parts of the stage not meant to be noticed, to which there was no need to pay any attention. Everything else went out, was muted; or at least, she, Mirta López, couldn't think about anything else, or keep track of anything else but that lean, grown-up youth, big to her because he was already sixteen, with his slow, serene walk, a metronome and, at the same time, the metronome's perfect needle, intangible, irreproachable, self-evident, substantial.

All this, which was no small thing, was why she felt the need, and more than a need, an urgency, to go to church to confess. Because the things that were happening to her, and which the priest had named childish over-excitement, imbuing them with innocence, no longer simply happened to her, just like that, some alien thing that seized her, like a rain shower catching us by surprise when we're out on the street and soaking us, like a dizzy spell that overtakes us and makes us go limp. Not anymore. Now she, Mirta López, with her questioning and with her thoughts, with her wiles and with her intentions, was a part of the matter: she would prepare for it, she sensed it, awaited it, imagined it and recalled it, got her hopes up mentally and then mentally recreated it. And no, she had not told anybody. She'd told nobody, but not like in the beginning, says my grandmother, who said nothing because it didn't seem, strictly speaking, as though there was anything to tell; and yet knowing, knowing deep inside her heart, that there was:

that there was something, a fervour and a passion, and that if she didn't tell anybody, as indeed she didn't, it's because it was no more nor less than a secret. A matter that was very, very much her own, that she could not or did not want to reveal to anybody.

But God sees everything, says my grandmother, the good Lord hears everything, and then, yes, then it really does make no sense to keep quiet or to feign. She went to church to confess. She thought she would say all of this. That was the only thing she had in her mind when she entered San Patricio's, letting herself be embraced by the building's graceful arches, walking down one side towards the confessional, crossing herself and kneeling down in the place of the mortified. But having begun to talk and to enumerate all these things, before the heavenly silence that was personified for her once again by Father Suñé, new details then appeared, truer confessions, which she hadn't planned to say, because the truth was that even she had not known them. She learned, in a way, at the same time as the priest did, she heard herself speak them just as he heard her.

Because, yes indeed: at the foretold times, she approached the dining room window, positioned herself on an armchair kneeling on the seat just as she knelt now on the wood, but then leaning on the backrest, against the smooth but firm velvet of the back of the armchair, looking outside; and when what she so fervently awaited finally occurred, when the Videlas' eldest son appeared from one corner or the other, depending which one's turn it was, she was filled with an undefined heat and that same deep shivering in her belly, and at that, amid that, yes, she squeezed, as much as possible, her lower part, while her torso, at the window, feigned impassiveness; nothing above, but everything below: she squeezed, pressed down, once, twice, three times, more times, she no longer counted; she pressed herself against the armchair, relaxed and pressed again, relaxed and pressed again, that is, in short, she rubbed herself, yes, rubbed herself, rubbed herself against the armchair, smooth and firm and also hot, looking out at the street as the Videlas' eldest son passed by.

Father Suñé, silent and still, became inscrutable to my grandmother. She had to wait a little to find out how he was feeling. Flustered? Furious? Forgiving? Or simply remote?

'You were rubbing yourself,' he asked or confirmed: my grandmother wasn't sure, and she's much less sure now.

She said yes.

'And what exactly did you feel while you were doing it?' he asked then.

Mirta López stopped to think. She said, finally: a tremor. The word was difficult, not altogether suitable for her age. And although she, very evidently, was no longer a little girl, she feared that Father Suñé might suspect a deception. Which was why she added: a fire, and then rounded it off: I felt a kind of fire. Later she thought, or she thinks now, that she was saying fire where previously she had said whirlpool, which was the same, or almost the same, as having said water. But the priest didn't care. He accepted, he took the thing about the fire.

'And what did you do with that fire? Did you try to put it out?'

My grandmother hesitated. Her poor metaphor was quickly turning towards the literal. Father Suñé pressed on.

'Did you try to put out this fire using your own hand?' he asked. 'Did you put your own hand in there, trying to put out that fire?'

My grandmother Mirta said no. Oh no, she said, no. The truth of the confessional.

'And wicked thoughts, did you have any of those?' Father Suñé continued. 'Did you succumb to lewd thoughts?'

Mirta López did not know, as yet, what lewd thoughts were; but she sensed that she hadn't had them, so she said no. Or rather she presumed, one might even say by common sense, that, not even knowing what they were, she surely hadn't had them. And so she said no.

Father Suñé declared that the Evil One had the most varied resources at his disposal, and lurked, as a rule, around the most innocent souls. By way of an antidote, deploying the formal tone with which a doctor prescribes a preventative medicine to a patient, or the corrective impress with which a schoolmaster assigns a pupil to copy out the word he's misspelled twenty times, Father Suñé informed Mirta López, my grandmother, that she was to pray three Our Fathers and then three Hail Marys. He concluded with a phrase in Latin which she, who had no mastery of the language, didn't even try to decipher.

Father Suñé, having completed his priestly task of confession for that day, would have started to pray, he would have spent a good while praying, right there, in his church, the church of San Patricio. He would have entreated, on his knees, for the salvation of all souls. In particular, he would have thought, but to think at that point is to say, because to think at that point is to pray, of those souls who are the most exposed, the most fragile, the most sensitive, the most tender.

Mirta López, that night, when it was time to go to sleep, knelt beside her bed, brought her hands together to pray, and said this: 'Our Father, who art in heaven / hallowed be thy name. / Thy kingdom come / thy will be done / on earth as it is in heaven. / Give us this day our daily bread / and forgive us our trespasses / as we forgive those who trespass against us / and lead us not into temptation / but deliver us from evil. / Amen.'

Once, twice, three times. After each one of those times, she crossed herself.

And then, next: 'Hail Mary / full of grace / the Lord is with thee / blessed art thou / amongst women / and blessed is the fruit of thy womb, Jesus. / Holy Mary, Mother of God / pray for us sinners / now and at the hour / of our death. / Amen.'

Once, twice, three times. After each one of those times, she crossed herself.

Then she remained in silence, motionless, thinking about nothing. Her eyes closed, in a state of absorption. Hands together. She felt her knees, on the dry wood of the floor; she felt her elbows, on the fluffy blanket of the bed. It occurred to her that she was adopting now, in the intimate solitude of her bedroom, the same position, or almost the same position, as in the church of San Patricio when she was confessing. But right away it also occurred to her, correcting herself, that she was adopting, really, the same position as on the armchair of the dining room of her house, the position for looking out the window, for watching the street.

Attributing to it the colour of a lion, following Borges's wise suggestion, is the best thing you can do for that disagreeable river. That is to bestow upon it a dignity, even a majesty, that it quite clearly lacks. Because, no: it is not lion-coloured. Nor are lions, in their bodies or their manes, the colour of this river. The river is too brown. It's the colour of what it is: it's mud-coloured. Dirty water and pestilence. This same brown colour, set amid rough vegetation, becomes intense, even wild (and it is not, even then, reminiscent of lions). That's what happens with the Paraná, seen from Corrientes or seen from Rosario. The Río de la Plata, on the other hand, which becomes total landscape, which allows no surroundings but itself, provides nothing but that brown that is so dirty and so ugly. Earthy brown, if you're being optimistic; otherwise sewage brown, rust brown. A feat of redemption, this discovery: to have written that it is a lion-coloured river. And another significant contribution, also from Borges: relating the city's founders to the simpler waters of the Riachuelo; not to these others, of la Plata.

In order to make a virtue of a lack, to invent another quality for this lack, Saer then named it: 'The river without banks'. Another discovery. And an enigma, because from what vantage point would you need to look at the river in order to see it like this? From the middle (no, that wasn't it) or from the air (which is what he did). It only works if you say it like that, using that plural, without banks (not like that house of Borges's which didn't have a 'pavement opposite'. Borges's shores, otherwise, are never the banks of a river). A miracle like

Guimarães Rosa's, with his 'third bank of the river', does not fit these waters, mediocre as they are; saying it like that, without banks, the way Saer said it, is glorification enough, it suggests exceptionality, a quality that is unique and very much its own.

We should add, too, that great title-maker Eduardo Mallea, with his 'City beside the unmoving river', a perfect formulation of fixedness and stagnation. First the city, stuck beside the river. And then the river, which rather is stuck in itself. The oxymoron, for once, is not a mere creation of language; reality itself supplies it, connecting the fluvial with the still, the flow of water with motionlessness.

Saer was from Santa Fe: a territory of pure riverbanks.

Borges from Buenos Aires: the city with its back to the river.

And Mallea from Bahía Blanca, which went further, which is more extreme: which turned its back on the sea.

Father, I have sinned. Mirta López was direct, emphatic. She said this with no circumlocution, no hesitation. She knew it: she had sinned. And she knew, she was fully aware, what they were, these sins committed. She could specify them, and indeed she did. The first: she had lied. The second: she had cursed. She had spoken false words and she had spoken dirty words, all of them addressed to her parents (my great-grandparents). Which, just thinking about it for a moment, could well in turn have entailed a third sin: disrespect to her elders.

'What curse words did you use?' enquired Father Suñé. He would not countenance any vagueness.

My grandmother Mirta replied: I called them sons of bitches. Then she mitigated, or thought she was mitigating: I said it without thinking. And she explained, seeking to be understood and not seeking to be pardoned for it, that she'd been overtaken by fury, that rage in her was overflowing. As she told the priest all this, activating her memories, something of that rage, to her great inconvenience, was returning to her.

'And the lie?', Father Suñé wanted to know. 'What was the lie you told?'

I said I had a really upset stomach, said, says, my grandmother. That my tummy was hurting terribly. That I really wanted to vomit. She told Father Suñé, that is, she confessed, that she'd even gone into the bathroom, that she'd leaned over the toilet bowl, that she'd stuck her fingers deep in her mouth, pulled down her tongue, trying to trigger the vomiting. All she got was two or three attempts at retching and a sudden burst of coughs that revealed her failure. And all for what? Because she didn't want to go visit the Zanabrias, not even to see Clara (who, yes, had been her best friend throughout her childhood; but now she thought her an idiot). Mirta doesn't know whether her parents believed her or not, if they guessed that she was pretending or accepted her ailments; but in any case, they decided that a bit of an upset stomach was not enough of a reason to cancel a visit that had already been arranged, that she could perfectly well go and only have a light lunch and then have tea with everyone, which would do her good, and skip the desserts and the tarts, easy enough.

Then Mirta López, in desperation, swore at them: she called them sons of bitches. Because inside she was calculating, while they were laying out to her, unmoved, these deranged reasons, that the train from Buenos Aires, the one that had left Once station that morning, would already be headed towards Mercedes. And on it, of course, on one of the seats in one of the carriages, looking out seriously over the fine fields, the reliable fences, the distant skill of some horse-rider, the Videlas' eldest son would be coming this way, returning home for the weekend, from the school where he was a boarder, he'd get off at the station, walk along the platform, he'd head towards his house following the same route as always, he would pass, then, right by her window, impeccable and sober, unimpeachable and austere, and she, she herself, Mirta López, would not be there at that window, would not look out and would not see him. Because at that moment she would be, conveyed by Miguel Ángel López and Benicia Vega, her parents, that couple of sons of bitches, playing some idiot game (hopscotch? elastic?) with that idiot Clara Zanabria.

Father Suñé understood that my grandmother was not confessing her fury, let alone easing it, but reproducing it: repeating it before him. And so he cut her off and pronounced: five Our Fathers, five Hail Marys. My grandmother Mirta started to cry. Right there, in the confessional. Not out of any feeling of guilt, of course, since she didn't feel guilty; but at reliving in her memory the feeling of infinite impotence from almost that entire Saturday, lunch and tea, all spent on this whole Zanabria thing, a victim of her parents, caged within the family and its rites of sociability, forced to spend the time, no longer with Clara, whom she already detested, but with the final remains of her own childhood, which she detested too. Hanging on the hours, knowing with infuriating exactness the moment of the day when the Buenos Aires train was arriving in Mercedes, and she absent from her essential place, squandering her surest happiness.

'God knows what He is doing,' declared Father Suñé.

Then Mirta López switched off her crying, from one moment to the next. The magical effect of his beneficent words? Father Suñé wavered. Some terrible storms, apparently certain, also dissolve into nothing, fade away as though devouring themselves, opening the way for that sparkling sun that they seemed to have buried away up there; or also, for that matter, the way certain drizzles, wearily persistent, as absolute as their overcast sky, suddenly open up with a cleft right in the middle, rending themselves from one side to the other like a taut piece of cloth when an initial incision has been made, interrupting their forever and opening the way to the light and the brilliance and the sky-blue. And thus it was that Mirta López stopped crying. God's handiwork?

God's handiwork, yes: God's handiwork. Because Mirta López, my grandmother, spent that fateful Saturday trapped by her parents, amputated from herself. Stuck in somebody else's house just as if in somebody else's life; subjected to the worst of alienations, the one that springs from one's own family, subjected to the paradoxical violence of affection and care. She returned home too late, when everything had already gone by (what everything is this? One thing only: the Videlas' eldest). The pavement, bare and meaningless, with nothing to offer but the first fallen leaves of autumn, looked apparently innocent, out-of-place or oblivious. The window of the house was pure frustration at that hour, the lowered blind (they lowered it, of course, whenever they went out for any length of time) giving it a horrible air of mutilation and burial. The armchair she relied upon, vacant and neglected that evening, reminded her of a playground swing, of a swing or a slide, seen at midnight, spied in the small hours of the morning, unreal and unreachable, the remnants of some other world.

But God does indeed know what He is doing. He knows everything and He sees everything. And He hates, more than anything, injustices. And this was an injustice. That Saturday, that whole Saturday, was nothing but pure injustice. So Mirta López, my grandmother, not fearing or suspecting that Father Suñé might interrupt to reveal to her, or to remind her, that God moves in unfathomable ways and that seeking to discern his plans is, in itself, another sin, just kept on going, out of sheer enthusiasm, out of an eagerness to tell more than to confess, to relate to Father Suñé that the following day, Sunday, was an anniversary, the tenth, of the death of Pedro Vega, Benicia's father, the grandfather (as he had been) of my grandmother (which she was not yet), and that therefore, in order to honour and commemorate him better, to entreat for his holy eternal rest, it was decided they should attend Mass at the Mercedes cathedral.

And there the three of them went, parents and daughter, on the Sunday morning; they walked across the square, beneath the invisible celebrating of the birds, and finally entered the cathedral with sober steps and prudence, Miguel Ángel pressing his hat to his chest. Mirta López looked and she saw. Amid the rippling of the town's parishioners, she sighted, constant and crystalline, the Videla family in full: the father, Don Rafael, in his uniform; Doña Olga, the mother, ever so devout; the eldest son, Jorge; his younger sister, the next brother. She acted purely on reflex, owing to which, for this reason, it could even have seemed spontaneous (but it was the opposite: pure intention). She sped up, actually guiding her parents, and took her place in the seat immediately behind where the Videla family were already positioned.

Mass is a ceremony of fellow feeling, of profound absorption, of profound connection with the other parishioners. The Videlas' eldest son, seen from behind, his severe profile espied from such a tight, anxious angle, seemed unreachable. Strange, thought my grandmother, says my grandmother, because she'd never had him so close, she had never looked at him from so close. The window of her house, she now understood, functioned for her like a cinema screen, the frame for a contemplation that was apart and without reciprocity. Now, in the town's cathedral, just a single row away, there they both were, the Videlas' eldest and her, Mirta López, on the same plane of existence, in the same dimension of reality. Would he know who she was? The Videlas were well known, in part because the father, Don Rafael, had been commander of the 6th regiment for several years, and in part, and even more so, because of that terrible misfortune of the death of the twins. But what about the Lópezes? Miguel Ángel López with his fabrics supply business? And Mirta López, his only daughter? Were they known?

The unwavering hair of the Videlas' eldest son, cut close and visibly kept in order with Glostora or with

Lord Cheseline, moulded his head with silent resolve. The hair looked so firm that it gave firmness to everything else: to his gestures, to his profile, to his shoulders, to his back. It wasn't the sort of hair for combing, like others, which gets altered, but hair for smoothing, for running a hand serenely over, knowing that afterwards there would be no hat, no cap, no wind that would be enough to shake it. The collar of his white shirt, ironed and starched, looked every bit as solid, without soft spots or creases. That shirt collar made you want to touch it, to run the tip of a finger along its edge; the fixed hair was very tempting, too, but at the same time, in its perfection, inhibiting. And between the hair and the shirt, between the close cut and the starch, the nape of his neck, of course: the neck. The admirable nape of the Videlas' eldest son, which brightened up before her eyes with the pride of a forehead or of a face. And this nape, straight and solid, did shine with the luminosity of a forehead, it expressed the assumed reliability of a face. Might this, Mirta wondered, be the reason why she directed her eyes, as she did direct them, forward? To lean in, pretending, to try to see, sidelong, a bit more of that face, a slice of that profile?

The moment for standing up arrived and then the moment for sitting back down: the Videlas' eldest son seemed to be made of steel. When he knelt to pray, lowering his head for the prayer, the nape of his neck shone and tightened, it lit up like revelations, it suggested transcendence. She shivered. An ecstasy of divinity overtook her and she brought her hands together to give thanks to God. Otherwise, by any other name, all of this would not fit into her body, nor would it fit into her soul. The Videlas' eldest son crossed himself with a conviction that surpassed beliefs; he stood and crossed himself, he bowed his head or rearranged his hands, with the contained vigour of a truth that she, Mirta López, had never witnessed before nor felt so close in all her life, her short life, she could have assessed it then, since she was only twelve, her whole life, she could say, she is almost saying now, now that she is over ninety.

Father Suñé, steady in the confessional, intoned a lengthy spiel of praise to the power of God. He rounded it off with morals. He adorned it with biblical figures. Finally, he gave my grandmother his blessing. And she understood that, with this, the encounter was over. She crossed herself, sat up and thanked him. She left the church almost at a run.

Father Suñé would have remained where he was a long while, alone with himself, which in this case is as much as to say with God. Perhaps somebody else might yet show up to confess. But it wasn't this that had kept him back, strictly speaking, at his confessor's post, so much as a certain feeling of shelter, or of refuge more than shelter, of great care, of protection. It was the same feeling he experienced the moment he stepped inside any church, wherever it was, and all the more when he stepped into his own one, if you might call it that, the church of San Patricio, over in Mercedes. That little booth of carved wood, devised to weaken secrets and reveal the concealed, would have proved for him at that moment an envelopment of guaranteed protection, almost a church within another church. He would have felt that he could remain there, and even stay and sleep there, hidden in the shadows like a traveller who takes refuge on the road, at night, deep inside a lay-by shelter. He would have thought of how awkward it would be if some other person were to find him crammed after-hours into the confessional. He would have agreed to leave this place for that reason only.

My grandmother was not at all sure whether she ought to carry out the admonitions prescribed by Father Suñé. He had said it, that much was certain; but he had said it in the middle of the confession, not after her deposition had ended. At that point, the main part of what she told him was still missing, the part with the Mass, the part with the devotion. Might she not suppose, perhaps, that this other part, the second, made up for the first? Might she not suppose, perhaps, that, more than this, it cancelled it out? But given her uncertainty, she opted to pray. Better too much, she thought, than not enough.

So she said: 'Our Father, who art in heaven / hallowed be thy name. / Thy kingdom come / thy will be done / on earth as it is in heaven. / Give us this day our daily bread / and forgive us our trespasses / as we forgive those who trespass against us / and lead us not into temptation / but deliver us from evil. / Amen.'

Once, twice, three times, four times, five times. After each one of those times, she crossed herself.

And then, next: 'Hail Mary / full of grace / the Lord is with thee / blessed art thou / amongst women / and blessed is the fruit of thy womb, Jesus. / Holy Mary, Mother of God / pray for us sinners / now and at the hour / of our death. / Amen.'

Once, twice, three times, four times, five times. After each one of those times, she crossed herself.

One word in particular kept going round and round in her mind: the word 'womb'.

Because she had first said stomach. And then she'd corrected herself, or thought she had, seeking to be more accurate and more precise, and said belly. But no, she was wrong. It was another word: womb. Although she was not at all sure where it ended and began, in the reality of the body, that word.

Had there not been a mistake, in reality, right from the start? If, as is customary, one can consider Solís the start, with his arrival, his little ships. Might not that whole story, of the river and the city, have begun with a mistake? Solís would not have gone into that unusually wide mouth if he hadn't thought, precisely because of its breadth, that these waters that he'd found led without any doubt from one ocean to the other, from the Atlantic to the Pacific. He assumed this: that he had, at last, reached the passage so longed-for, which would make it possible to cut through, to save time, to make transportation cheaper, to pass quickly to the other side (because America, the continent, turned out to be, simultaneously, a discovery for them and an obstacle, both a destination and a stumbling-block).

He was wrong. A fiasco of islets and watercourses from the north made the poor man see, sooner rather than later, how badly he'd messed things up. He wouldn't be getting through this way, it was nothing but this side. He resigned himself. He invented a name, he called it the Freshwater Sea. It wasn't bad: a vast body of water, like that of the sea, but without the salty air. And yet this baptism, which was excellent as a metaphor, was ultimately false. Freshwater Sea? Neither sea, nor fresh. As a sea, it was lacking everything, not only the salt: the colour, the movement, the attractiveness. And in its taste, in its unimaginable taste, if it did occur to anyone to try it, it was bitter as mud. It was bitter because it was mud.

The indigenous people killed so as not to die, and they ate for that same reason. The name that came later, though it stayed and still endures, also has something mistaken about it. Río de la Plata? But it's no river: it's an estuary. A wide entranceway or a mouth for others, which really are rivers. And de la Plata? That silver believed to be there, a false promise by the water, riches that didn't exist, which explains why nobody ever found them. The silver remained only in the 'Plata' of the name, or remained in name only. In the name of the river, via a direct route, and of the country, via an etymological one.

The river, much later, had its city and its port, each with its own respective name. The fact that the city's name ended up being the name that had been the port's, and that its own had meanwhile been totally lost into nothingness, says a lot about the facts: what it was that mattered most and what it was that mattered least, or what it was that mattered and what did not. And then, of course, the city turns its back on the river.

It was Mass, the holy Mass, that revealed to Mirta López this divine possibility: of gazing at the Videlas' eldest son from close up. She had taken the separation and the apartness imposed by the window, thus far, as given, as irreparable. The house, her place (the house and the armchair, of course); and his, obviously, the street. Was it not him, perhaps, a bit older now, was he not the one who always came and went, studying in Buenos Aires, while she, more constrained or more restrained, just remained in Mercedes? And yet, of course, things could be different. She learned this at the cathedral: she was not banned from approaching him. A pretext or a good reason could always be invented. Or pure chance could also be invented, mere coincidences, why shouldn't they? Luck doesn't exist, she'd been taught that in catechism: everything is God's work. Why, then, should she not work on her own luck and fabricate an accidental encounter with total premeditation?

She knew the exact time the train arrived from Buenos Aires at the Mercedes station. She could calculate how long it took the passengers to get off, to populate the platform, to drain away. She could time – and in a way, secretly, she already had – the minutes required by the unvarying itinerary of the Videlas' eldest. Instead of positioning herself, as was her habit, on the armchair of the dining room of her house, at the window, to watch him coming past, what she did was to go out onto the street ('Where are you going?' Benicia asked her; 'I'll be right back', she replied), taking the same route as him, only in the opposite direction. In a block or two, at most, she was sure of it, she would run into him.

Anybody watching from above (and who would watch from above but God?) would be able to anticipate the encounter. And so could she, but she had a doubt: would he be coming along the same pavement, so that when they passed she would see him close up, or would he be coming on the opposite pavement, so that going out wouldn't actually have done her much good? The coin in the air and the spinning knucklebone flashed through her mind. Just then she saw him approaching. Upright and regular, a little less than a hundred metres away; and on the opposite pavement. Heads, tails, upward, down. She considered this a test by God: one must surrender to fate; but also work it, a little. Pretending (but pretending to whom?) suddenly to realise that the grocery store she was apparently visiting was not on this side but the opposite one, she crossed the paved street almost at a trot, like a clock whose hands are being wound forward. The hundred metres must now be sixty or seventy. And the Videlas' son, their third and now their eldest, was coming straight towards her.

There was something, she thought, of the chess bishop about him. Even though his walk conjured straight lines, not diagonals, more like a rook, then. A reed, a pillar, a mast, an obelisk? He was not solid, nor especially tall; but to her he suggested firmness, inflexibility. She focused on his sweater, navy blue. Seeing it subject to the evidence of his torso, one would suppose it quite impossible to wrinkle. Held in trousers that were ochre or beige, via a broad and reliable belt, it captivated her, it dazzled her, that blue sweater drew her in. She couldn't run towards it, no: that would have given her away. But her heart did start to beat harder. And her legs (how could she have run like this?) started to tremble a little. She focused on his white sneakers. He wore white sneakers. She thought, as she kept moving forward: he could walk through soot, he could sink into the mud, kick ashes, and his immaculate white sneakers wouldn't stop shining like that, immaculately white.

She crossed one street, he was coming now, they were going to pass each other at last. She could see him: close up, and face-on. And how about him, did he see her? Did he look at her? Did he notice her? He gave every indication that he did not. His eyes kept their gaze up high and forward, expressionless. As for Mirta López, not only did this not disappoint her, but it was what ultimately lit her up. Seeing him so haughty while also humble, so within her reach yet so far above, she looked at him with such intensity as they passed, that it was incredible he did not, in turn, reciprocate the look, if only for that reason. That moment, fleeting and conclusive, made her feel, without quite knowing why, that her life was going to change for ever. A sparkling, a dazzle, a radiance, an annunciation? All of that, yes. On a dull corner in Mercedes, two blocks from her childhood home, on some unremarkable Saturday morning.

He passed her and walked on, towards the Videlas' house, towards hers. She, meanwhile, her mouth dry and her body damp, checking her dress and her shoes, fearing that something about her wasn't, hadn't been right, checking that yes, it was, she maintained (for whom? for herself) her tenuous sham of a trip to the grocery store. She wasn't going to retrace her own steps, going back after the Videlas' eldest son, that would have been foolish; in fact, she did not even turn around to see him. What for, if she had seen him already, close-up and entirely, now and forever? She kept on going, towards the grocery store. And when she reached the grocery store she went in. And not only did she go in, but she bought: a bar of chocolate and a half-kilo of little water biscuits. She returned home with this. Retracing her own steps? Not only that. Also the steps, so recent and so palpable, of the Videlas' eldest son.

Coming back into her house, the everyday scene she encountered became totally unbearable: her mother in the kitchen, starting to prepare lunch; her father just back from work, dealing with his Saturday half-day. She was indescribably irritated by all this trivial normality, after having lived through what she'd just lived through. She felt expelled by this alarming shallowness called family, so she left her shopping on the kitchen counter and went wordlessly to her bedroom. But she didn't cry. She didn't cry because the desire to cry, which, in a way, she did feel, got inexplicably mixed up with a huge feeling of joy: all together, all within her. And isn't that, in fact, how whirlpools are formed: from the clash of two opposing forces? And no sooner had she thrown herself onto her bed, face buried in the pillow, arms pressed to her body, than that whirlpool did begin, the thing that she, in the confessional, had called by that name. The image came into her mind of the Videlas' eldest son, just as she had seen him when she passed him on the street: the blue sweater, the white sneakers, the leather belt. Wicked thoughts? Were these, she wondered, the wicked thoughts? No, she told herself. What could be wicked about what had just happened in the middle of the street?

She pressed herself against the bed, pushing with her waist, as if she were on a beach, lying on the sand, and didn't want to be seen. She pressed and then released. She pressed again. Released again. The whirlpool gradually turned warmer, inside her, like any element that spins and, in spinning, starts to produce heat. She pressed and released, her waist pushed into the bed, pressed and released, pressed and released. She thought: the sweater, the sneakers, the belt. She thought: the nape of his neck. She saw everything, she pictured it in a memory that, being instantaneous, did not seem to be entirely a memory. She bit the pillow. She sank her face in, just as she did her waist, and bit into the softness. At what point did one metaphor start racing towards the other: how did the whirlpool come to stop resembling a whirlpool and start to seem a fire? She was suddenly short of breath, and supposed it was because she had her face in the pillow. But she moved her face aside, opened her mouth, and still she was breathing heavily.

She cannot remember whether the idea of the fire had occurred to her, in her attempt to explain what she didn't know how to explain, or whether it had been put to her by Father Suñé, perhaps to suggest, by association, the idea of hell. At this point, however, what did it matter? There she is: right in the fire. Rubbing herself against the bed, biting the pillow very hard, and driving in her nails, too. The sweater, the sneakers, the belt; the nape of his neck, his neck, his neck. A fire whirling, in the middle of her. In her stomach. In her belly. Or, rather: in her womb. In her womb, yes, in her womb, Mirta López thought, Mirta López discovered. This wasn't exactly the stomach, like when you eat too much; nor exactly the belly, like when you're nervous. That was it, it was the womb. The same as when you say the fruit of thy womb.

The womb, the fire, the hand. Because a fire like this one, metaphorical and not literal, doesn't get put out by throwing water on it. Nor by covering it with blankets. Not by blowing on it, either. This fire was figurative and it was happening inside her. She brought her hand to her womb, to put it out. Her hand beneath her body, her body pressing against the bed. Or her hand against the bed, her hand pressing her body? The sweater, the sneakers. The neck. The belt. The fruit of thy womb. The hand presses and the body rubs itself. That's how it happens with fires: first they grow, intensify, expand, become vast; that's how they react, at first, to water: as if it were firewood, as if it were gasoline. And so it was in her, Mirta López. To begin with, more burning, more heat and more breathlessness. She said something without meaning to: she didn't know what, she doesn't know what. She bit her lip, like the pillow before it. She felt she was expanding and simultaneously contracting. And only afterwards, thanks to her hand, the flames began to go out, the fire ended.

When her mother called her to lunch, she was a different person. The usual question, had she washed her hands, sounded stupid to her. Of course she'd washed them. With soap? With soap, yes, with soap, and not before sniffing them a little. They had lunch chatting about trivialities, exchanging gossip from the town. Small town, big hell, concluded her father, a great fan of the obvious. She listened to everything from far away. She felt different, she was different now. They ate chicken with mashed potatoes. For dessert, a crème caramel. She still remembers.

To Father Suñé, predictably, what had occurred seemed very bad. She sensed him turning in his narrow confessor's spot, as she recounted the things that happened. He puffed as he listened, and contained his anger as he spoke. The implicit pact of discretion and privacy that constitutes confessional work suddenly seemed to founder, including in its foundational condition, that of mutual invisibility, even if she knew that the person to whom she confessed at San Patricio was none other than Father Suñé, even if he knew that the person confessing these aberrations was none other than López's little girl, it seemed to be suddenly in peril, because Mirta López truly got the impression, and with that impression felt a fear, that Father Suñé might come out of his place (leave his little box), appear before her, approach her and slap her. Which, since it was him, would still be, strictly speaking, a sort of punishment from God.

But he didn't. Father Suñé heard her confession, as pre-determined; at the end he spoke in turn, identifying sins and severities, rigorously and harshly though never raising his voice, and finally pronounced not his verdict, which could be taken as understood, but his sentence: he hit her with ten Our Fathers and also ten Hail Marys, demanding that she repent and that she never, but never *ever*, relapse in her actions.

Father Suñé would have felt so mortified to learn of the terrible straying of one of the best cared-for sheep in his flock. Because despite not being, since they were not, one of the most devout families in Mercedes (they went to Mass sometimes), the Lópezes were very good people, very proper, very decent, and their only child, little Mirtita, had grown up in a quite suitable environment, safe from the temptations of evil. With some of the other girls in the town, the goodtime girls or the foul-mouthed ones, he might have been more forewarned, knowing them more exposed to vice. But he would have felt unsettled, as well as rather agitated, at Mirtita López's situation, and her such a little girl otherwise, such a good little girl and therefore so fragile, so naïve and for that same reason so feeble when faced with the ferocious stalking of Beelzebub.

He would have imposed on himself, as shepherd, the due penance. He would have deprived himself of food that same night, he would have fasted. To honour God and to contribute, with his own suffering, offerings and simultaneously redemption, to the swift correction of Mirtita López's stray soul, her rapid return to the path of righteousness. He would have prayed for hours. He would have slept very badly.

Mirta López, my grandmother, alone in her room, late at night, knelt to pray. She prayed: 'Our Father, who art in heaven / hallowed be thy name. / Thy kingdom come / thy will be done / on earth as it is in heaven. / Give us this day our daily bread / and forgive us our trespasses / as we forgive those who trespass against us / and lead us not into temptation / but deliver us from evil. / Amen.'

Once, twice, three times, four times, five times, six times, seven times, eight times, nine times, ten times. On finishing the whole batch, because even the mere idea of alternating made her feel lazy, she crossed herself.

And then, next: 'Hail Mary / full of grace / the Lord is with thee / blessed art thou / amongst women / and blessed is the fruit of thy womb, Jesus. / Holy Mary, Mother of God / pray for us sinners / now and at the hour / of our death. / Amen.'

Once, twice, three times, four times, five times, six times, seven times, eight times, nine times, ten times. On finishing the whole batch, because even the mere idea of alternating made her feel lazy, she crossed herself.

The repetition had put her almost into a trance: the litany, being a litany, produced a kind of hypnosis in her. And when she went to lie down, turning off the bedside light and covering herself up, she noticed that the repetition didn't stop, that some of those many mangled words were still bouncing around in her mind. She heard 'full' echoing. She heard 'amongst woman'. She heard 'of thy womb'. She felt an echo: 'thy womb, thy womb, thy womb'. She played around, she cut it up: 'The hour of our.' And also 'A monk swimming.'

She had fun, she thinks she even laughed. She fell asleep happy.

A few days later, she was turning thirteen.

Back in a very other time, and on the Costanera Sur, the hordes used to gather on the bank of the river, less to escape the heat than enjoy it. There was a spa, or a kind of spa; it might have been an imitation of the beaches in Mar del Plata, but nobody seemed to mind, since ultimately the river, all things considered, was itself no more than an imitation sea. They squeezed enthusiastically into those tight-fitting breeches, with flounces and no sleeves, that were the swimsuits of the day (not swimsuits; bathing suits: that's the more appropriate name), and they got into the still hospitable water. Water that was muddy? Certainly; but fresh and desirable in any case, the whole summer long.

The ban on bathing in the Río de la Plata was enacted in the sixties, owing to the high degree of contamination of the waters. The industries of the suburbs, not entirely thriving nor too numerous, did nonetheless discharge, with absolute thoughtlessness, tons of waste into their nearest river basin; the Riachuelo, mainly, though also the Reconquista. They seemed constant and efficient in nothing so much as in this energetic dedication to poisoning; they seemed to produce nothing as much as they did waste; their industrial waste was the most industrial thing about them.

The Riachuelo and the Reconquista empty into the Río de la Plata, which also found itself poisoned soon enough. Contaminated waters, rotten waters, lifeless waters, pestilential waters, and nobody else was to bathe in them. People withdrew and learned no longer to think of them. What had been a spa became ruins. And

Buenos Aires, a city that was dry.

The toxic substances emitted by the industries killed almost everything in those waters. Death prevails in the most decisive manner of all: making life inviable. As if to ratify the sign of death, or rather recognising it, criminals would toss into the Río de la Plata the defenceless bodies from their killings. Why, then, not think of it as a weak flank? Why not try to get in precisely through there?

The modesty of her few years, and of what was just beginning, made her reserved: nobody, with the exception of Father Suñé, learned what was happening to her (now, though, her many years have reversed the mechanism: all modesty in her has faded away, so she speaks absolutely openly). She began to form habits. The window one, for starters, had already become a whole ritual. She had not shaken this habit because it allowed her to unite things: to consider those correct steps and put out her own fire, all at the same time. Those were the advantages. But there were disadvantages, too. Condemned to the dining room, because her bedroom didn't overlook the street, she was unavoidably exposed to her mother suddenly coming past, or even her father coming past, if he arrived back home a little early from his business or got up a little early from his siesta. These sudden intrusions, and even the expectation of their mere possibility, spoiled everything a bit, broke the spell in a second (they put out any fire more quickly than her hand, but in doing so, they left her out-of-sorts: all jumbled up).

Since the year was progressing towards the phase when days were colder, it was necessary to wear more clothes (pullovers over blouses, full-length stockings under dresses) and for those worn to be thicker (cloths and wools, flannels). Mirta López, at the window, as she watched the passing, in his austere splendour, of the Videlas' eldest son, pressed herself against the armchair or resorted discreetly to her pacifying hand, but now she felt her body a little distant, a little out of reach. At night, when she went to bed, getting hastily under the sheets and blankets, she had made her discovery. Because the nightdress that covered her, with its weight and its flounces, would inevitably run up her body, if she got into her bed quickly, and would be left mostly rolled up at her hips, at her waist. She didn't always feel like rearranging it, pulling it back down. Why not sleep like this?

Although she was leaving her childhood behind, proud and nervous, my grandmother still felt, especially on the darkest nights, her old fear of nightmares. Sinister dreams of rabid animals on the loose, of being locked in a cellar, being forgotten by her parents on a dingy street of some uncertain foreign city: things like that. The trick of falling asleep thinking about purely good things, so that the dreams would turn out good, too, had always worked for her. Except that these purely good things, which over the years had consisted, for example, of castles for princesses or car drives with her father, today took just one form: the serene, secure walk of the Videlas' eldest son. Was there anything in the world that could inspire greater confidence?

That, however, as she was well aware, was precisely how the fire started. So these good thoughts, could they be wicked at the same time? Once again, she couldn't decide. And once again, she would have to check. With the palpable memory of that walk, accessible but unengaged, there began the tingling, the whirlpool, the sparse warmth, the breathlessness. Her hand would move down, as if of its own accord, as if moved by somebody else, and found no nightdress: nothing but her legs, her blessed womb, a thin bit of silk, a light bit of fabric, easy to crush, even easy to move aside, her body was changing, and so she was changing, too. Her other hand, the clumsier one, which was no use to her for writing or cutting either, she would use to cover her mouth. Because she had, lately, ventured her mouth upward, and in such cases she used to moan, and in the total silence of the house, in the discord-less silence of the deserted streets of the Mercedes nights, no moan from her mouth should be heard: it must not, because she could not explain it.

The joy of the window did not, however, exclude, and it had no reason to, the option of going out onto the street. Mirta López went on doing it, from time to time; whenever she felt the desire for that other experience more strongly, of walking right past the Videlas' eldest son (following him, she doesn't know why, was something she never thought to do. It never occurred to her, simple as that. It didn't cross her mind). She would go out to find him, that is, to meet him, with the arrival of the train at the station; she would always see him at more or less the same point, a bit before or a bit after the very same corner. She even felt the hopefulness (first she thought it was fear, but no, it was hopefulness) that on one of these times he might even recognise her, that he might give some indication that he did; a good-neighbourly nod, a glimpse of a friendly smile, at least a quick glance, anything. She would know how to be receptive, and perhaps also responsive, too. But the Videlas' eldest son walked with such a regular gait (imitated, perhaps, since childhood, from his father, Don Rafael), that nothing seemed to have the power to alter it, neither in its rhythm nor in its trajectory; he had his eyes stilled, cold, already definite, incorruptible, neither lost in nothingness nor focused on any point in particular, but resting upon the world, like a hand upon a table, like a boot in a stirrup. As she passed him and moved away, in any case, without having, apparently, even been registered, she felt no disappointment, nothing that let her down; quite the contrary: these were the happiest, fullest moments in Mirta López's life, as well as a kind of factory that would generate, as night-time approached, those good thoughts that would make her sleep better, relaxing first her body and then her deceitful mind.

She became a regular at Mass, too: another proof of virtue. Because her parents, irreproachable in their faith, went only occasionally to the cathedral on Sundays, they went for anniversaries and other special dates (the Feast of the Immaculate Conception, Good Friday, Palm Sunday, St Cajetan, Christmas), they were not among the permanent fixtures. But they saw, of course, approvingly, that their only child, their daughter Mirta, after her Confirmation, gave herself to that fervour of attending every single Mass (they did say they'd go with her, but the subject faded). She would go alone, all dressed up: there at the church, she argued, she would meet her girlfriends, that wholesome camaraderie of towns and parishes would take shape.

And when she was there, she did indeed meet Francisca Almada, and Clara Zanabria, and Graciela Vázquez or María José Beltrán; they would talk for a bit on the pavement, or sometimes in the square opposite. Once inside the church, though, she preferred to sit alone: it helped her to fully engage, to give in to the situation. The Videlas were always there. Always, always; they were all there (father, mother, the three children. The eldest came back from Buenos Aires almost entirely for this: to be at Mass, with his family). Formal and circumspect, opaque but luminous, you would think it was them, simple parishioners, who, just as much as the children's choir, the forceful sermon, the light filtering through the stained glass, defined those Masses' atmosphere.

Mirta López managed to sit, each time, as close to them as possible. They were bearing a tremendous tragedy, everyone knew it, the inconceivable deaths of Jorge and Rafael; but not only did they not look struck down or shaken because of this, they very evidently exhibited a sober, eternal temperance, which nothing now could break. From Mass, of course, they were never absent, and for her, my grandmother, it produced a special fascination to bear witness, as the centre of the scene, from a position that was so to speak privileged, to the ascetic devotion of the family's eldest son. The figures depicted in the church, she suddenly realised, had something of that same almost sovereign neutrality, reigning over innocent joy (the Christ child in the manger, lately arrived) or extreme suffering (the redeemer nailed to the cross, bleeding, agonising, redeeming), the greatest tenderness (the Virgin contemplates the boy: the fruit of her womb, Jesus) or total devastation (the Virgin contemplates the fruit of her womb, Jesus, detached, so very pale, limp, dead). Each of them there and at the same time, somehow, farther off: always a bit farther off.

On some weekday or other, her father needed to travel to Buenos Aires. Formalities, arrangements, procedures. He took her with him. This is the kind of thing that gets recorded for ever, my grandmother remembers it still. She'd been in Buenos Aires before, of course; she knew it, knew that it was endless, that it could not be encapsulated. That it was not only taller, faster and more intense, but also more unlimited than a place like Mercedes; that even those who lived there mostly didn't know one another. And yet she took to thinking, with a kind of certainty that can only be called faith, that once she was there, amid the buildings and the buses, amid the advertising billboards and the million passers-by, she would meet him: the Videlas' eldest son. Don't they greet each other, actually, Argentinians, if they happen to run into each other in Europe, if they hear each other talking and recognise each other on some street in Madrid, in some café in Paris, some museum in London? Thus they too, she reasoned, and reasoned well, would greet each other, recognising each other, the Mercedinos, if they happened by chance to meet in Buenos Aires.

She looked greedily at the countless passing faces: walking along the pavement or carried by the cars, in the windows (she looked at the faces and at the napes of necks: the one she yearned for, no doubt, she'd be able to recognise among the throng). At one point, she plucked up the nerve to ask her father: Are we far from the Colegio San José? Her father frowned, rubbed his chin. No, he said. Not far. My grandmother did notice the vagueness of this answer, but that didn't stop her from telling herself that 'not far' meant 'near'. And in that near (but how near? how not far?) was the certain hope that they were going to meet, that she was going to meet him.

It didn't happen. And on the way back, on the road and in the car that her father drove in silence, while the evening was falling and the lights were starting to come on at various disparate points, Mirta López, a little sad and a little dazed, wanting to cry and to get into bed as soon as possible, spotted, in the middle of the countryside, the determined passing of the train. It contented her, it consoled her, to be watching, like this, the journey that the Videlas' eldest son carried out time and again, the plains he ploughed through, the landscape he saw. She pictured him on the train, on that train, though knowing he couldn't be there at that very moment; she imagined him sitting stiff in his seat, straight-backed, looking at the countryside, the route, the cars. It was as if they were passing each other right now, out of nowhere, car and train, the two of them, the way they passed each other on foot, on the street, back in Mercedes. Mirta López got excited.

It was only many days later that she told herself it would be good to go to confession. She felt, so to speak, at peace with her conscience. Her life, albeit with some new habits, seemed to have stabilised at last, her dreams were calm, her mind did not torment itself. If there were fires, she stifled them; and going out onto the street, as she was wont to do, to fabricate innocent coincidences, was not at all out of keeping, in her opinion, with other similar games that were entirely appropriate for her age. She showed up to the confessional without anything very definite to say to Father Suñé. She knelt down to recount, in that sacred place, before a priest, almost as she might have done to a girlfriend at the Delicias de Mercedes cake-shop, the latest matters in her life.

And yet, she was wrong. Father Suñé listened to her discourse, imbued with an apparent abstention; but in reality he was taking great pains to separate the many scenes from the tangle of her testimony, the way an inspector or a taster might do it, an appraiser or an expert, when separating lesser jewels from true gems, fake papers from good bills. He set aside, by means of a non-engaging muteness, her coming to Mass, the trip in the car, the outings to the grocery store, the train going past. He spoke only when Mirta López fell silent, when she was left with nothing more to say. 'And how about your hand?' he asked.

My grandmother answered with metaphors.

But Father Suñé loved concreteness, precision, he loved exactitude.

'Where do you touch yourself? How do you do it?' he enquired.

Calling things by their actual names? But my grandmother didn't actually know what things were called.

'The womb of the fruit?' the priest got angry when he heard her.

My grandmother floundered, she spoke nonsense, she felt lost. She burst into tears, she says, and she seems to discover, now, with some interest, that the phrase includes the verb 'to burst'. She begged forgiveness. She curled into herself.

'Do you put your fingers inside?' asked the priest.

Mirta López said nothing.

'Not in your womb, sinner! No, your pubis, your vulva. Do you put them inside, wayward child? Do you put them in?'

Mirta López was crying.

Father Suñé let her know that she had committed very grave sins. Mortal ones. And repeated ones. Which maybe even God would not forgive. He enjoined her to return to the way of virtue, to repent her sacrilegious behaviour, to pray fifty Our Fathers contritely, and fifty Hail Marys. He did not absolve her, as he had on other times; he punished her: 'May God forgive you.' And he ordered her to leave.

Father Suñé would have shut himself away, wide-eyed and almost tearful, in the secret truth of the cloister, he would have taken off his cassock and his coat to be left just in his shirt, his thin shirt, that was all, and underneath that, his vest. He would have grasped the wooden handle firmly, he would have shaken its leather and its harsh tips. And he would have begun to scourge himself. Dry blows, sharp, necessary, undeniable, that hurt his shoulders, that hurt his back, that gave him pain as he prayed, that made him suffer in his own carnal wretchedness; to find out whether this pain and this suffering of his might save a soul.

Once, twice, three times. Ten times, twenty times. The words rebelled, they would not allow themselves to be repeated. Mirta López uttered them, her hands clasped, her eyes shut, with true devotion. But how many times can one say the same thing, always the same, without starting to say something else? She heard herself and was unnerved. 'Half Arthur'? 'Harold be thy name'? 'Unearth our cities in heaven'? 'For givers are trespassers'? 'Hey, Mary, full of grapes'?

She sensed that all this, too, was a serious sin: she was wicked. But she wasn't the one responsible, or was she? The words changed all on their own, beyond her intention. Fifty was too many times. The phrases were not so amenable, it was them that kept getting away from her. 'Hail, merry fool of Grace.' 'Thy condom, come.' 'Forgive us our pressed-asses.' And so forth. Until she fell asleep.

But the most emphatic way of denying the river does not consist of, as they say, turning one's back to it. There is another way, which is more precise: gaining ground from it. Gaining ground from the river has been and continues to be the most consistent recourse for trying to eliminate it and making Buenos Aires a city that is Mediterranean in appearance. Land instead of water. The gullies are still there (in Belgrano, in Parque Lezama) but they descend from the ground to the ground, they're no longer the banks of anything. The river retreats and is becoming ever more distant. And it becomes ever easier to assume its non-existence.

Why advance, however, with earth in that direction, as if the city were short of room, when you have, on the opposite side, the famous vast pampa, the enormous desert, the immeasurable plain, an infinite surplus space? Tossing earth and more earth onto the flattened, still river, isn't that actually, in a way, an attempt to transform it into pampa? More and more flat land, less and less water. Adolfo Prieto has already written about the fruitful usefulness of the English travellers' maritime metaphors for those writers of ours who, in the nineteenth century, travellers in their turn, but above all else readers, took to describing the pampa. The pampa as being like sea: the land like water. Wouldn't gaining land from the river be the opposite operation, opposite and complementary? Wouldn't it be an inversion of the metaphor, passing through it into literality? The river as pampa. The river turned pampa.

Treading upon the river, riding over it, crossing it

on foot, going across without boats or swimming. This impossible became possible, and no longer just in a metaphorical sense, nor in the habit of tossing earth onto it, nor in a miracle like that of Moses (open waters), or a miracle like that of Jesus Christ (solid waters). There was once an extremely marked historic drop in the water level, the product of a tremendously strong wind; the waters began to withdraw, exposing the riverbed to view. Mud that was soft, gummy, flexible, unstable; but still ground and not river. This low water level, which was so extreme, made it possible to mount a horse to cross eastward to the Uruguayan side.

The story that Rodolfo Walsh was writing, when they took him away, was about this. Then the criminals burst into his house, to loot it and steal his things. They took his papers, too. The story was never heard of again.

As time passed, of all these habits, it was going every Sunday to Mass that started to give my grandmother the greatest satisfactions. While the confessions murmured in the San Patricio church became increasingly sporadic, irregular, Sunday mornings at the Mercedes cathedral held firm, with the constancy of a fervour. The whole town, or slightly less than all of it, in any case the lion's share, noted this assiduousness, superior even to that of her parents, all of which was transformed into a generalised fondness towards her: they would smile benevolently, approach to greet her.

The Videlas never missed a Sunday either. The five of them from the family, as if they really were just one. They always sat together, unified; not so as to avoid mixing with others, but rather to confirm their perfect unity or to have it seen by the whole world. The eldest son had already finished his secondary studies at the Colegio San José in Buenos Aires and he had, in March, going contrary to the preferences, seemingly puzzling ones, of his father, entered the National Military College. He would leave there on Saturdays, but arrived for his visits to Mercedes a little later than during the previous phase of his studies. He didn't travel, as he had before, on the Sarmiento railway branch, but took, along with fellow students who also lived to the west of Buenos Aires, the number 57 bus, managed by the Atlántida company. He changed at Luján (Mirta López knew Luján by heart: the basilica, the esplanade, the council building, the bus terminal, the riverbank, the river; hence she was able to imagine the scene with testimonial precision).

My grandmother had a scare the first time she failed to meet him; she imagined, for a moment, that he had given up on his family visits every weekend; she wondered, now in some distress, whether this renunciation would mark the beginning, owing to age and, perhaps, to new forms of social interaction, of his not coming so often to Mercedes. She suffered in secret and without good reason: it wasn't like that, that wasn't it. She soon came to know (in a small town, everything is known, no inquiry of this kind lasts long) what the new conditions were, the new rules: the bus from Luján and its timetables (a bus station was something Mercedes didn't have, not like the railway terminus; but an almost central square where the buses, when they came in, stopped to let their passengers off. What could be strange about her, Mirta López, such a bookish and solitary girl, so diligent and so reserved, going to sit with some book on a bench in that square? Who could possibly notice, however much she might be concentrating on her reading, that the arrival of each bus, its rockslide engines, its squealing brakes, the door groaning open, so to speak, might distract her, making her look up?).

Mass was the one unmissable date, that much did always remain intact. Mirta López, my grandmother, arranged matters each time in such a way as to position herself, among the faithful, not too far from the Videla family. And preferably behind that line that they, so perfectly together, drew when they sat down. My grandmother managed, as I say, as she says, to sit not too far from them, and often, more than this, she managed to be very close, no more nor less than in the very row behind. Did it just seem so to her, or was there in the eldest son, who by now had turned seventeen, who was already living a military life, an increase in smartness, in sobriety, in distinction, in straight lines? Was she inventing this, by suggestion, or were his hair and his movements, the nape of his neck and his posture, improving their limpid aspect? His shirts, better than the sweaters, accentuated with their stiff collars the overall effect.

On the Sunday when my grandmother arrived at Mass (the door to the church, the ample pavement, the square opposite) and didn't see the Videla family, she felt like she was dying. Could it be? She was trembling as she went in and wanted to cry. She sat down and told herself that today she was really going to pray properly. To pray and ask God for nothing bad to have happened, for the habit of these meetings never to be harmed. There was no need, she never got round to praying. Either that or her private entreaty of despair was equivalent, for God, to a prayer, and Mirta López's prayer was answered. Because the Videla family, delayed by some matter that no longer had any significance, made their entrance, at last, into the cathedral. She saw them sidelong, out of the corner of her eye. Once again she wanted to cry, but now at her good fortune. Yes, they had come. And as if her disordered requests had deserved to be granted total satisfaction, it happened that the Videla family not only showed up, arrived, came in; but that the five of them sat, in a formal and thought-out progression, in the very same row where my grandmother was sitting. And they did it in such an arrangement (the two older men, father and eldest son, at the ends, as if protecting the younger son and the two women) that the eldest son happened to take his place right beside my grandmother.

The Mass began with a sermon about the fatherland and its values: the month of July was approaching, and within that month, the ninth, the anniversary of the declaration of independence. This followed by a well-measured explanation of the dangers of the breakdown of these values, of these and all of them, with a precise enumeration of solvent factors: from sexual promiscuity to the scourge of alcoholism. Then people had to stand up, to sit down, to stand up. To repeat prayers in an echo, to ruminate over private supplications, to sing in the modesty of the choir. To raise eyes to heaven and to close them for better insight. To request and to thank. To repent any ills inflicted and forgive those ills received. To give thanks to God in his unfathomable triplicity: Father, Son, Holy Spirit.

Mirta López couldn't turn to look at the Videlas' eldest son. But she could see him in a way, a mixture of direct perception and intuition. And more than that: she knew he was there, so close, beside her. Something better than seeing him, as she'd been seeing him for so long already, on the square and in this church and on the streets of Mercedes. Something better than seeing him: she *felt* him. She felt his presence, right there, beside her. Together, yes, or almost. He was doing the same as her at the same time as her. Not only keeping time with her, but also united, in each successive step in the ritual. Mirta López couldn't decide which of the factors made her happier: whether it was the sweet simultaneity or the miracle of finding themselves so close.

The tingling seemed to start in her stomach, and the heat in her knees. Tingling, thought Mirta López, or also bubbling, or perhaps fluttering. Heat, she thought; like you get in the summer. But she also thought: burning. In her stomach, in her chest. In her knees, in her thighs. How could she know? Many things, and in her body. She felt as though the thick air was passing through her mouth; to get in, to get out. It never entered her chest at all. She parted her hands from prayer to rest them on her own face. It was warm. Possibly flushed. The Mass enveloped her in a protective aura. The cathedral's images (faces with eyes turned upwards, a half-open mouth, the enigmatic smiles of sexless winged children) comforted her, too. The Videlas' eldest son beside her, close to her, *with* her.

Mirta López contracted: her shoulders, her arms, her legs. Also her belly, also her womb. She contracted in order to turn each part onto itself, as if each one could cause friction, not with the others any more, but with itself. She felt she was coming apart, which was why she contracted, which was why she squeezed herself; she sank but into herself, she entered but into herself. Cradled in holiness, she was happy to be breathing. Never in her life, absolutely never ever, had she felt so devout. But with a devotion to what? The Videlas' eldest son, almost visible, was a certainty, the most complete certainty. And she beside him, without moving, was turning around; still on the outside, she turned. Eyes turned upward, mouth half-open. Body squeezed.

She was wearing a woollen coat, because a new winter had begun. A long one in a colour that she had called brown but was terracotta. She hadn't taken it off in the church. The scarf she had: she'd taken it off and placed it, all tangled up, onto her lap. She touched the back of her neck: it was damp. Her legs probably would be, too. And maybe also the whole of her was. In the middle of herself, something like the middle, the highest curve (but simultaneously the deepest) of that disturbance. Then she, Mirta López, put a hand into one of the pockets of the brown or terracotta woollen coat. Because that brown or terracotta woollen coat had two generous pockets in its lower part. Into one of these pockets (the right), Mirta López put a hand (the right). She rested it on that part that she understood as the middle of herself. She held it down hard, she pressed.

There is a rhythm to praying, a cadence; this comes, like everything, from the Jews, who mark it with their bodies when saying their prayers. This rhythm went through my grandmother, to her hand. The hand, placed first in her pocket and then in herself, went on pressing and pressing, stirring up what's already stirred up, with a rhythm that was regular but growing in intensity; hidden in the pocket, in the wool of the coat, clandestine in the colour that she didn't quite know how to name, invisible but complete, evasive but certain, she was pressing against herself and moving in a very tight little circle, in a distance without a journey; a point (a single one), and in that point, the universe; the kingdom of heaven in the earthly world; the height; the heavenly, conquering the part down below; rhythm, cadence, scansion, do you not mark them with your hand?; the hand in her pocket, the brown or terracotta pocket, running over her, not to her side; running over her, more or less in the middle; her hand like a dervish, spinning and then still; her body suffered (suffered?) a spasm, contracted and released; Mirta let an 'ah!' escape; she disguised it, a clever trick, into an 'amen'. She bit her mouth. She looked over to the side.

'Go with God,' said the priest, from the pulpit.

And they did.

Absolute happiness prevented her from asking herself, on that day and on those that followed, what she thought about what had happened. She was able to conjure it up, she could do that, and in truth she never stopped doing that, and she could also mimic it (she did this almost every night, in secret, in her bed, raising up her night-dress), but she could not think about it. An epiphanic glow enveloped her memories, imprinting upon them the irrevocable stamp of an absolute goodness. How could she have sinned in a deed of such spiritual upheaval? Surely she had not. It must be something like those saints' ecstasies that had so fascinated her since she was a girl. There was nothing more precise, and as the same time, more indescribable. About her condition, about her experiences, she could declare no more.

She told herself this, my grandmother says, but at the same time, very deep down, there was something bothering her. She did not go to confession, and there was some reason she didn't. She found some new excuse at each moment, urgent matters that got in the way, tasks that occupied all her time. Eventually she had to admit, however, that what she was truly doing was avoiding appearing with the truth and before the truth. When she did notice, she made herself go to the San Patricio church and present herself before her confessor. This time she did not prepare, as was her habit, mentally, a summary of her human frailties, nor did she sketch out, as on other occasions, a brief outline of what she was going to say. This time, in the confessional, without rehearsal or premeditation, she allowed the words to carry her.

And the words, for some reason, did not carry her to the Mass on that Sunday in the Mercedes cathedral. They even kept her away from there. It was not that she stayed quiet or actively refrained from mentioning it. No, it was simply that the words started taking other paths; they wove their journeys in very different directions. She confessed, for example, in the process of confessing, that she had not completed, in time, the total number of Our Fathers or Hail Marys that had been imposed upon her as a penance. But to this, Father Suñé replied with uncommon humour, quite unsuited to a confessional, that sometimes, when it came to large numbers, even God can lose count. What was important was not the number, the matter of an exact science, but the fact of there having been contrition and sorrow, a weight upon the soul and a recanting.

Mirta López later wondered about her omissions. What good would it have done to keep quiet, even if unintentionally, if God is all-knowing? Omniscience, omnipotence, they mean exactly this: that He could know it all. Mirta López calmed down: if He could know everything, He could also forgive everything. Because if not, then He wasn't omnipotent at all. She told herself this, and crossed herself.

Father Suñé would have felt pleased, relieved. Virtue, once again, had vanquished vice. His prayers and penances and the mortification of his own flesh had risen to heaven and touched divine mercy, all for the good. The sheep that had once gone astray was returned to the flock. The good shepherd's duty.

He would have been left calm and happy. And shortly afterwards he would have learned, because very nearly the whole town learned, that Mirta López, the Lópezes' girl, had a boyfriend. A nice little boyfriend, yes, perfectly normal for her age. And that this boyfriend, this nice little boyfriend, was not (this seemed preferable to him) the Videlas' eldest son. It was not him, but another; a slightly bigger lad, from a farming family, who he learned was called Anselmo.

It is not only the river, however, or it is not so much the river as it is those many other watercourses that furrowed the city and, in a way, furrow it still. We pretend they don't exist, that they never did. The city imagines itself being as solid as it is arid; that famous humidity, which maybe even defines it, dissolves like a mere thing of the air, only a thing of the air. Of the ground, nothing is said. And of the underground, much less still.

And yet there they were, and to tell the absolute truth, there they still are, those many little rivers and streams that ran down its slopes (because the city also imagines itself as being very flat, an urban pampa, and it is not) and that now flow, though now in pipes, beneath its ground. In a fiction of non-existence even more convincing than that of the river, people live as though there were none of this.

The streams, however, do exist, beneath certain streets. Namely: the Maldonado stream (under Juan B. Justo), the Vega (under Blanco Encalada), the Medrano (under Ruiz Huidobro and then García del Río), the White (under Campo Salles), the Ochoa-Elia (under the Nueva Pompeya neighbourhood), the Cildáñez (under Suárez, Cárdenas, Avenida Remedios, Lasalle), the Manso (under Pueyrredón, Sánchez de Bustmante, Gallo, Austria), the Granados (under Perú and then Bolívar), the Matorras (under Independencia), the Ugarteche (under Juncal).

They flow unnoticed, forgotten down there. They are not lost, but transformed. Now they are our sewers. Mostly they flow into the Río de la Plata, at a spot that's not too far from the airport, or else directly there.

They're used for disposing of waste.

Anselmo Saldaña first approached Mirta López, my grandmother, beneath a half-open tree on the Mercedes club waterfront. The youth of the city used to go there to entertain themselves, and my grandmother, by then, was soon to turn fifteen. Some would take out a rowboat, others played soccer or basketball. Others simply went there in order to lie down in some bit of shade, on top of a soft piece of fabric that allowed the noble coolness of the lawn to come through. The well-chilled drinks and the meaningless laughter helped to pass the time. And pass it did.

Although my grandmother, by inclination, was quite a reader, she failed to interpret, to begin with, Anselmo's ways of courtship. She had no guile, nor did she ever suspect any. She supposed, out of pure innocence, that the dreamy looks Anselmo gave her were mere drowsiness, that the silences he reserved for sighs and melancholy were mere lulls in the conversation, that was all. On one occasion, he brought a changeable hand nearer to touch her hair, and she, startled, asked him if there was something there: a burr, a spider, something like that. She thought he wanted to correct her.

Anselmo, however, had his strategies. He had more of them than of anything else: a more than well-stocked arsenal. He arranged things, time and again, so as to be left alone with Mirta, making the constant group of their friends evaporate into nothing; he managed to get near to her, to talk to her from close by, to brush against her clothes. On one occasion, acting as though they were not in fact alone, he whispered something in her ear, as though a secret, because supposedly that's what it was, could only be conveyed with all its body language. He was twenty: more than five years older than her. His father Don Emilio's chicken business extended to include, within the town, a poultry store that was very well regarded, and, beyond the town, a commercial supply circuit for Buenos Aires. Anselmo took care of that. He was a symbol of prosperity.

Mirta López's innocence did, in theory, leave her at the mercy of Anselmo's wiles; but it also, simultaneously, armoured her entirely against them. Because, being so innocent, she was quite unaware, she allowed him to advance, to lurk, to prowl; she allowed him to insinuate, suggest, strike verbal blows. And at the same time, for the same reason, none of this had any effect on her. She didn't respond: neither favourably nor unfavourably. She didn't accept, but nor did she refuse. She did not welcome, but nor did she repel. As simple as that: she did not respond. And she didn't respond because, on the whole, she had no idea.

Anselmo Saldaña was, by then, and possibly from the outset, hopelessly (as they say) in love with Mirta López. He liked everything about her, and he liked this everything so much that the parts he didn't know (her way of being, for example) he could only imagine he would like, too. He knew she had no boyfriend, and that she'd never had one. He was correct, then, in a sense, attributing to shyness both her abstention and her reserve. And he was correct to think, not encountering in her any obvious dissuasion, and there being no rivals in view, that it was only a question of time and he needed to be able to wait. But waiting like this, with no defined timeframe, was becoming impossible (something completely impossible and, at the same time, his only option: the only thing left to do and what he could not do).

Mirta López's faint apathy, while absolutely not a strategy, was ultimately equivalent to one, in that it was equally effective. She only just consented, only just allowed; but always giving the firm impression that she was aware of nothing. In a way, she let things be done; but in a way, she didn't seem to notice that there was somebody (Anselmo Saldaña) doing something (trying to seduce her). Watched hungrily by the poor wretch Anselmo, Mirta López did not give up the least indication of what was happening inside with all this prowling around. She seemed neutral: neither flattered nor annoyed, neither hopeful nor distressed, neither haughty nor overwhelmed. Available, but elsewhere: she let things be done.

Anselmo, who was a little cautious, asked around her closest female friends (Francisca Almada, Clara Zanabria) for some clue to her private thoughts; but no, there was nothing, my grandmother was extremely reserved (was that it – extremely reserved – or was she hiding something? Or was she not hiding anything because there wasn't anything, because abstention, that divine abstention, was her whole truth?). She now says she doesn't remember, she reckons she wasn't thinking anything at all, that she was living hollow, her mind blank, her soul still. Having Anselmo around did not bother her, not at all; nor did he attract her. Perhaps, in a way, she did like him. In any case, she did not feel the slightest need to show him. Not that, nor anything.

It is understandable that, with an attitude of this kind, she had ended up getting Anselmo Saldaña to fall in love with her, even madly in love. How long could all this last? When would this thread snap, from being stretched and stretched and stretched? Anselmo took to thinking maybe never. That this suspended state in which he was living, combining afternoons together, twilight strolls, blossoming chats, happiness, could be protracted indefinitely. There were some threads, or there could be, that were capable of not snapping ever. Then a day came, a day like any other, with a breeze and some clouds, the club nice and peaceful, him quite moved, her with a blue ribbon in her hair, on which Anselmo Saldaña approached Mirta López, looked into her eyes, waited for them, and once she, silently, looked back at him in turn, albeit expressionlessly, he told her that he loved her: that he was in love with her.

Mirta López said nothing. He realised it would stay that way. And he understood that this silence, if he let it be prolonged, would end up being transformed into rejection, however much this might not have been what she intended. So, after declaring himself, he moved towards her and kissed her on the mouth. A resolute kiss (more resolute than him, the person giving it) whose duration indicated to him (not without some private anxiety) that she was not opposed. Because she didn't pull away, didn't push him, didn't feel overwhelmed: she let herself be kissed, first, and then she agreed to kiss too. Wasn't it strange that something so immensely anticipated (by him) could prove simultaneously unexpected (by her)? And wasn't it strange that, this being so, he seemed to find it so incredible that it had occurred, while she, judging by her expression, seemed to take it quite naturally? They looked at each other a second. Anselmo smiled, as if asking a question. And Mirta, as if answering, smiled too.

It wasn't after the kiss, but during it, that my grandmother managed to wonder what it was that she was feeling: whether she was liking or disliking what was underway. The subject had come up, more than once, among her girlfriends, as an exchange of views, or of conjectures, between those who were on one side or the other of that firm border called experience. Very well: so now it was happening to her. And she had felt neither curiosity about it nor any anxiety. Very well: so this was it. It was happening to her. A man's mouth on hers. A man's tongue and saliva (opinions divided: 'how revolting'/ 'you don't even notice') in her mouth. This was it. It was happening to her.

Was she liking it? Yes, she liked it. This is what she said: she liked it. Pleasure was an altogether inappropriate word, eagerness would be going a bit far. But as for liking it, yes, she did. She liked it the way you talk about something you've tried and that you accept will happen again. In that sense, yes: she liked it. She felt pleased not to have been repulsed, but also at the very fact of having been kissed. And she did not manage to consider, neither then nor later, whether what she'd liked had been the kiss, kissing, being kissed or Anselmo Saldaña: the one who'd kissed her. Weren't they in fact the same thing? That kiss and the person who gave it were one and the same to her, inseparable by definition. From the fact that she had liked the kiss, she inferred that she liked Anselmo Saldaña. And since she was unaware of the existence of shades, scales or progressions, or had no interest in considering them or disentangling them, she told herself, maybe happy, that since she liked Anselmo Saldaña, then she was in love with him.

Having kissed him, for a start, or having kissed, with him, did in fact mean that they were boyfriend and girlfriend. That's how it was to her, that's how it was to him, that's how it was to her girlfriends, to the kids at the club, and that's how it was to everyone in Mercedes (there did exist, of course, those who kissed without being a couple or without becoming a couple: they were the town sluts, and you'd find none of those in her circle). The news of the courtship was well received by everyone: by the group of friends ('it's about time'), by her father ('I'd like to meet him'), by her mother ('he's a good catch'). Even, and especially, by Father Suñé, who explained that love, when kept pure, is always a blessing from God (that was what he said: 'blessing').

Anselmo Saldaña was a devoted man, supremely committed to his work, eager to progress, very sociable and a good friend. The future with him seemed assured. My grandmother sometimes found him a little dull (to be more precise: she yawned during their talks), but maybe that was the price to pay if you wanted solid prospects. He suffered from one vice only, and that was beer, which he drank to excess; at the wrong time of day (in the morning, for example) and at the wrong time of the year (for now, in the winter). The beer did, however, make him a bit wittier, which meant the tedium abated (thus had my grandmother learned that life is governed by a law of balances and compensations). She was still too young to start drinking beer herself: she wasn't allowed it, nor did she want it; but she did realise that, in future, beer is something she was going to like, because she already liked the taste that the kisses from Anselmo, her boyfriend, conveyed to her via an indirect route.

She got used to thinking of him like that, to saying and to having other people say that Anselmo was her boyfriend. She was not, however, getting remotely used to the way in which his shirt collars folded: they seemed always wet, though they never were; sort of damp, and weak. She was comparing them, of course, to those of the Videlas' eldest son: impeccable. Anselmo's warped according to his movements, soft and saggy; they warped or even rolled up, they made him look ugly. His hair got messed up — that made her apprehensive, too. He agreed, at her request, to smear it with gel, and she was hopeful that it would now look elegant. But that wasn't to be, now it was even worse. The slicked-down, precise hair of the Videlas' eldest son gave him an air of sobriety, conveying the absolute certainty that nothing would alter it (not his perfectly combed hair, and not him himself). Anselmo, on the other hand, had sinuous hair that, without quite curling, was certainly wavy. Pasted down with Glostora, it took on the appearance of wire. And instead of being compacted, like that of the Videlas' eldest son, to the harmonic shape of the skull, it poked out unexpected thorns, loose cables from broken appliances.

And the shoes, also the shoes. Those of the Videlas' eldest son made him look secure, well planted on the ground, and at the same time remote, a bit above everything; he trod decisively upon the world, but without touching it, never sinking down. Anselmo's rustic espadrilles, meanwhile, or even worse, the dilapidated moccasins with which he vainly attempted to mimic a certain elegance, were almost never free from stuck-on mud and grass. Sometimes it was dried mud, which would flake off as he walked; but sometimes, generally, it looked damp. Just like Anselmo himself. Because it was Anselmo himself who made her think of damp, of the damp of wardrobes, the damp of gutters. In contrast, and this was abundantly clear, with the lovely dryness of the Videlas' eldest son. Dampness, she specified, also suggested sponginess, lumpiness, gumminess, that vague evocation of milkiness. Unless she, Mirta López, just forgot all about the taut-fibre form of the Videlas' eldest son. But how was she going to forget that, if she didn't stop, despite everything, watching him go by on the street, and walking past him through false coincidences.

Nonetheless, she felt that Anselmo did love her. Which was why she allowed the relationship to last. The kisses continued, ever more passionate. And the caresses began, and she liked those, too. Over the clothes, at first, and under the clothes, later. Under the blouse, the back (but threatening to move forward); under the skirts, the legs (but threatening to move upward). The shrewder of her friends had already sounded the warning: boys always want to screw. But getting married without being a virgin was the worst possible stain (including to the men who, despite being the ones who caused it, immediately go on to despise that condition). Reaching one's nuptials immaculate (ah: so that's what immaculate was) was essential.

Anselmo accepted her proposals readily (so it was true, they had advised her well: if she allowed it, he himself, once she'd been screwed, would see her as a whore and wouldn't want to marry her). But he explained to her, in return, talkatively pedagogical, between kisses and endearments and murmurings at siesta time, that her hands were already no longer virgin, having held onto things before now. She could, then, with no fear of lapsing into sin, touch, grasp. And he explained to her, all set to explain, that she was not virgin in her mouth, because she had drunk and eaten, because she had licked and swallowed ('Do ice creams count? Does food count?' Anselmo: 'Of course!' Another doubt: 'And pee?' Anselmo: 'No. Pee doesn't count. Because it goes past without opening, without tearing through').

That was how Mirta López grasped and touched, that was how she licked and swallowed, preserving her virtue, intending to remain chaste. Father Suñé confirmed it: God permitted this satisfying of the man, because it served to protect purity. If it were some vice, it would have been a sin, and a serious one; but like this, on the contrary, it was proof of holiness. It served as an offering, even a sacrifice: granting the male these lesser reliefs, so that she might herself arrive untouched at the union under sacrament. Incidentally, he added, almost gladly, it also kept her from those wicked thoughts, which were the work of the devil, as well as from her self-absorption, a dreadful practice, which was merely the devil inside her own body.

The opening of the subway in 1912 (Plaza de Mayo to Plaza Miserere, the first line installed in all of South America) would, I presume, have created the illusion of dominating, through modernity and through technology, the world underground. Light and speed replaced, in the imagination and in fact, the realm of the catacombs.

Along with that illusion, this other one: that the streams that have been squashed, contained, suppressed down there, might no longer exist. Considering them no longer just culverted, but extinguished. And that the city of Buenos Aires went on, just like that, as if down below, there weren't holes and water flowing, an old water cartography, canals and hidden corners, silent tunnels.

But you need only peer into a cellar, for example, to confirm by the constant leaking, by the palpable looming of the years of damp, that the streams of that geography are still there. Or it's enough for it to rain, suddenly and in abundance, in Buenos Aires, for the water to spring up to the surface, to climb over the kerb, graze the houses, shake the cars, to re-establish old courses, to be restored to its open sky.

Ezequiel Martínez Estrada wrote that the pampa, crushed by the metropolis, denied by the city, was now emerging from the deep and conquering (reconquering) Buenos Aires. Something of that kind, of the same order, happens sometimes with the streams. When it doesn't, they flow in silence, it seems easy to forget them. Normal life unfolds on the surface, mentally abolishing that sub-city of dark and latent galleries. No one thinks of that underground. No one pays it any attention. But just see what happens up above when what's submerged re-emerges, when the clandestine city undermines the visible one, when the suppressed flow returns towards what suppresses.

The summer of '46: the Videlas went away en masse, as they usually did, for their holidays up in San Luis. Oh, they just loved that province, my grandmother says; they even thought of themselves as being from there; some relative of theirs had been governor a while back, a fact from which they obtained, with no great effort, a kind of lineage. The air in the place was good, as they said, and the mountainous landscape supplied periodic compensation for those months dominated by the total flatness of Mercedes. My grandmother's family (which is, at a greater distance, my own) had always preferred the sea: the windy bustle of the beaches, the weary whispering of the waves.

That particular summer brought changes to the country: one government replaced by another. There is an art to keeping lives constant, not allowing them to be altered by facts that are merely external. Nonetheless, says my grandmother, the general changes would change the lives of the Videla family, too. The father, under the new regime, would stop being the mayor of Mercedes. He would retire, as was customary to say in such cases, with the satisfaction of having done his duty. There would be other winds blowing, for him and for everyone.

This, however, was not the summer novelty that had the greatest impact on my grandmother. Fortunately Anselmo was around when the rumour arrived and spread across Mercedes: the Videlas' eldest son, over in San Luis, had met *someone*. Someone? It was understood: a woman. And him so temperate, so abstracted? Him so temperate, yes, so abstracted. He had met someone. Someone? A woman. Fortunately for Mirta López, good old Anselmo was still there, ever her boyfriend. And fortunately he did not ask why exactly her love for him had so intensified in that late summer, just as he had never wanted to know, either, what exactly was going through her head when she embarked upon ardours with him. She loved him more than ever, despite his being kind of greasy, despite his being kind of soft, because in those days she felt less sad than angry.

The news soon came through: the Videlas' eldest son, in the middle of their family vacations, had started to step out with one Alicia Hartridge. European blood, distinction, refinement, pronunciation. Mirta López hated the oilcloth tablecloths, the shabby espadrilles and the toothpick habit that made up, in part, her world. She said 'Hartridge' out loud, when nobody was listening, trying to find that intermediate point of speaking that exists between an *a* and an *o*, that exile of the *ge* that throws it out between the *ch* and the *y*.

Summers are denser: deeper, more sluggish. My grandmother, so she said, had always been puzzled that this time of year should be associated with lightness, fleetingness (when you say, specifically, that a certain romance is a 'summer romance'. To her, it was the opposite). The heat makes things more concrete, more solid. To which one must add, incidentally, the taste for the definitive that the Videlas' eldest son had always shown. She couldn't imagine him, Mirta López couldn't, taking any step rashly, nor taking a step backward. If Alicia Hartridge, as people were saying, was his girlfriend that summer, then she would be thenceforth. And on top of that, he would marry her. And he would have his children with her.

Which did, indeed, happen. The Videlas' eldest son married Alicia Hartridge on Saturday 7 April, 1948, two years after meeting her. He was then twenty-three years old and already a lieutenant in the ranks of the army. He had his children with her: three males, two females (the first boy, however, barely lived with them at all). By then, in any case, Mirta López had taken the precaution of marrying Anselmo Saldaña, my grandfather. She did it a year earlier: in May '47. By the time the other thing happened, she had her life all figured out.

My grandparents got married in Mercedes cathedral, but the parish priest who officiated at the ceremony was none other than Father Suñé. A specific request from Mirta López. The party, the following day: in the Las Violetas hall. They danced into the small hours, they ate until they could eat no more. The honeymoon: down in Bariloche. A whole week at the El Ciervo Guest House, with views of Nahuel Huapi lake from some of its windows. They went on excursions, they ate venison and trout, they swore to stay together their whole lives. And they did.

They went on living in Mercedes for a few years more. At the end of '53, they moved to Buenos Aires. They had three children: Ángel (my dad), Roberto (my uncle), María Cristina (my aunt). They had seven grandchildren: one by Ángel (a grandson, that's me), three by Roberto (my cousins, all boys: Julio, Mario, Eugenio), three by María Cristina (my cousins − a boy: Diego, and two girls: Marcela and Julieta). Once in Buenos Aires, they always lived in La Paternal.

My grandfather Anselmo died of heart failure on the first of June 1978, the day the World Cup started. My grandmother Mirta accepted her widowhood with serene dignity, with true resignation. In time, with the passing of the years, she started to experience occasional problems: she would fall for no reason, she'd forget things. A couple of times she was out and got lost, and didn't know how to get back home. One time, Roberto arrived to visit her and found her lying on the floor: she had fallen and she'd had a knock. At first, she hadn't recognised him.

The family (what was left of it) decided that the best thing would be to take her someplace where she would be cared for. *Old people's home* read the sign on the door, avoiding, as usual, the cursed term: nursing home. An old people's home? A house for the elderly. At least she would no longer be hurting herself or spending hours in distress wandering unknown streets (none of which, including her own, seemed remotely her own at all). They'd give her food without salt and her full complement of medication, without any negligent forgettings or muddling up one pill and another.

The old people's home, the house for the elderly, the nursing home, is called Plaza Mayor and it is on Calle Plaza in the Saavedra neighbourhood. My grandmother says she's doing OK there. I'm the one, out of everybody, who visits most often. Sometimes, when I arrive, if she's groggy or a bit out of it, she mistakes me for my father. She'll say, for example: 'My, you're looking young!' and I can tell that that's why. I don't correct her, I don't say anything. Over the course of the conversation, she realises of her own accord that, no, that it can't be, that I'm not.

II

AIRPORT

At seven a.m., the three of them go out. It is already light, because it's February. The sky has been clear for a while. They get into the van: two in front, driver and passenger, and the third in the back, the part for cargo. The floor in that section has already been fixed up. A sheet of metal, welded and riveted kind of roughly, is now covering what until recently was just an opening. Whoever is travelling in that part of the vehicle, in the back, no longer needs to grab on as they go. Or rather, they do, but only so as not to be jostled about, not so as to avoid falling into the hole. The hole is the perfect size for any one of their bodies to pass through. Indeed, over the course of a few days, all of their bodies had passed through it. To get out and to get in. To go down and to come back up. Then it had stayed, and it was a danger. When braking suddenly, or hitting a pothole, anyone who lost their balance and slipped in where the uncovered hole was, could end up right on the road, and break something, get seriously hurt, even be trodden on by one of the Citroneta's wheels. And worse than that, even worse: somebody might notice them.

It's seven, and they go out. The day has arrived.

They slept there, at Pepe and Érica's. The four of them had dinner together: Pepe and Érica, David and Martín. There's no room in the studio apartment, they figured it out as best they could, eating on the floor. And they figured it out as best they could to sleep, too. The cot, a sofa. The floor.

Over dinner, they talked about music. They talked, but most of all Martín talked. And about music but most of all about the piano. About the piano and pianists. Because Martín knew a lot about that: about the piano and pianists. He's a pianist himself. He plays really well.

He knows a lot about the piano and pianists, and he also knows a lot about explosives. He is admired, among other things, for this, because he combines that class of learning, that of a more refined culture, with clear practical know-how, which allows him to take action. All of them reject a choice of this kind, but not all of them are in a position to overcome it.

Martín is. They don't just enjoy listening to him talking about Gulda, Richter, even Maurizio Pollini. He didn't just help by distracting them, on the eve of the operation. He also instilled confidence. He also made them feel surer of themselves.

They chatted, they ate. Then they settled down to try to sleep. The night went by, dawn broke. It's now seven. They go out.

Martín is in fact the group leader. He is as a result of his standing and his prestige.

But also group isn't the word. And leader, if you think about it, isn't either.

Martín is lieutenant Martín. And the group is not just a group, it's the Benito Urteaga special unit. It is under his command.

The terms, then, have shifted. But everything has shifted. Names, too.

Because Martín, lieutenant Martín, is not really called Martín. He has an alias, they call him Auntie. But he isn't called Martín.

Just like Pepe is not called Pepe. He's not even called

José, which is what guys they call Pepe are called.

And David isn't called David.

Nor is Érica called Érica.

Everyone has adopted a new name.

And Érica and Pepe, who live together, as a couple, in that studio apartment on Calle Austria where they all ate and slept, aren't really a couple. They're pretending, that's all. They're pretending so as to give the neighbourhood that impression. But they aren't a real couple.

This way, the house looks trustworthy.

Friends can come over for a meal. Nobody is going to pay any attention to what time they leave, nor whether they do.

At night, while they were eating and chatting, something happened on Calle Austria.

The police set up a roadblock almost directly opposite the house. Those sorts of controls are common enough these days. A squad car is positioned partly across the street. It keeps its lights off. The officers are positioned on either side of the road, like a bolt ready to be drawn shut. They gesture to each car: to pull over, to stop. Then they take a good look at the driver and decide: let it continue on its way or inspect it. They tell the driver to turn the lights on inside the car and they watch closely. They can't trust anything: if there's a kid in the car, for example, if there's a little old man or a little old lady in the back seat. They can't trust anything. They ask for papers, for the car's documentation. They search, where possible, the trunk. They peer underneath the car.

They'd never seen a roadblock right there before, on Calle Austria. Usually they prefer to set them up on the main avenidas, where it's harder to slip into the side streets. But sometimes they go for the element of surprise.

They follow proceedings, from inside, without looking or paying too close attention. The cars would stop, the sound of voices, the noise of doors, the cars would drive on. They didn't interrupt their eating, they didn't interrupt their talking (specially Martín: about Horowitz). They didn't take it, at all, to suggest a bad omen; nor, even less so, as a cause for concern. They truly felt very safe, there inside the house. And they also felt very sure about what, the following day, they were going to do.

After a while, the police lifted the roadblock. Calle Austria went back to being calm and quiet, as it usually was.

The day came. They had been waiting for it, without knowing which day it would be exactly, since 19 July, 1976. Now they know: it is 18 February, 1977. Almost seven months had gone past. Now they know that this is the day they were waiting for, and that it has come at last.

On that July day, in the middle of the terrible winter, there had been a meeting of the leadership (of the new leadership: Merbilhá, Mattini, Gorriarán). And the most complete secrecy.

From out of this meeting there arose a slogan, a certainty: 'We've got to shake up the board.' Because the course of events was taking on a sinister nature; strictly speaking it already had. And if they didn't manage to knock things onto a different course, if they didn't manage to shake up the board, the defeat would become irreversible.

From out of this meeting there came not only this slogan, but also a plan.

They needed to strike at the regime, and in as extreme a way as possible.

Nobody mentioned, though it would be mentioned years later, the boldness of those who'd taken risks with Operation Valkyrie, the heroic place that history would reserve for Joachim Gauck. The inherent glory in making an attempt on the despot. Counterfactual? Quite the opposite: pure facts, pure action. Striking at the regime, shaking up the board, killing the tyrant, demonstrating power: all of this was said at the June '76 meeting. And a plan was established, too.

They were reluctant, as we know, to carry out attacks using explosives.

Attacks with explosives always involve the risk of there being innocent victims. And they were absolutely strict about the need to avoid such a risk.

Attacks with explosives were, furthermore, the sort of thing done by terrorist organisations, their preferred mode, their almost exclusive method.

And they, as we know, were not a terrorist organisation.

They were not seeking terror, rather the contrary. They were seeking to strike a blow *against* terror so as to inspire the people with confidence that they could fight against the regime, that it could be defeated.

It was a truly exceptional action, and this exception entailed another. This time, what they were planning was a greater attack, the greatest attack, and they would do it with two explosive charges.

Some fifty kilos of TNT, more or less. The idea had come from Auntie, which was Martín's nickname (the nickname of his alias, that is, because he wasn't called Martín). The whole plan was put forward by the Turk. The Turk wanted to plant just one single explosive charge; one single charge, not two.

But, no: they couldn't. They would have to (they had to) plant two.

At seven a.m. on Friday 18 February, 1977, the three of them go out: Pepe, Martín and David.

Not Érica. Érica does not take part in the operation.

She says goodbye to them and is left alone in the apartment on Calle Austria. That studio apartment where she pretends to live as a couple with Pepe.

In a little while, she will go out to work. She works at a textile factory.

She also took on this work pursuant to a strategy. That is not, however, to imply some pretence. Not at all, rather the opposite. She takes it on as a way of getting to the truth. To her own truth, you might say.

Érica is twenty-six.

It could have been another day. Not any day, but some other. Indeed they'd already taken their time waiting and weighing up, deferring and selecting. Until the day came, and this will be the one. Friday 18 February, 1977.

Because after 8 a.m. on this day, between 8 and 9 a.m. of this Friday 18 February, an airplane will take off from the city of Buenos Aires's Jorge Newbery Airport.

An airplane: a Fokker F28.

An airplane: Tango 02.

That plane will be carrying General Videla.

Travelling with him, among others, will be José Alfredo Martínez de Hoz (economy minister), General Osvaldo Azpitarte (commander of the army's V Corps), General José Villareal (secretary-general of the Office of the Presidency), Brigadier Oscar Caeiro (head of the Casa Militar), Guillermo Zurbarán (energy secretary).

The plan is for this flight, an official flight, leaving from the Jorge Newbery Airport of the city of Buenos Aires, to transport them to the city of Bahía Blanca, in order for them to take part in a series of ceremonial events and informal meetings.

Érica tears up the cardboard boxes that the previous night's pizzas had come in. She puts the torn scraps in a plastic bag. She ties the bag expertly with a knot. She puts it under the table that she uses for cooking and for eating, when they don't eat, as they did last night, sitting on the apartment floor.

She hears, meanwhile, coming in from the street, the unmistakable sound of the Citroneta's engine. She hears it starting. She hears its sound for the minutes it takes to warm up. She hears it make the effort to get going.

Érica stands in front of the small, slightly stained mirror that's hanging from a wall. She tidies her hair with a clasp before going out to work. She works in a textile factory.

Érica isn't called Érica.

The security measures employed in such cases are tough, rigorous. The checkpoints, unbreachable. A joint operation by the police and the army. The area is overflowing, hours in advance, with blue-coloured squad cars and olive-green-coloured vans. Ford Falcons and Ford F100s. Also some jeeps. Also motorbikes, which come and go. And officers on foot, prowling about.

Traffic is cut off on the Avenida Costanera, the only main road allowing access to the small Jorge Newbery Airport. It's cut off on one side and on the other: on the north side, the one with the strip of restaurants and the university campus, and on the south, the one with the port and the lorries. There are barricades and there are vans positioned crosswise. Soldiers with rifles are stationed across the avenue, and also on the pavements (the one beside the river and the one beside the airfield). No vehicle may pass. Not for any reason, and with no exceptions.

There are no parked vehicles, because the ban on parking or stopping, subject to the warning 'the sentry will shoot', is permanently in force. No car stops ever. It wouldn't occur to anyone.

On this side, the access side, the closure is secured.

Same thing at the ends of the runway, which no cars would reach, because the traffic, well before this, is being diverted.

On the other side are the tracks of the Belgrano railway, protected by harsh wire fences. And the straight, single line of the cleared Avenida Lugones, which has also been closed to traffic (diversion via Calle La Pampa).

The morning flights, those departing as well as those arriving, have been postponed till after Tango 02 has taken off and left the airfield.

The passengers on those flights, even though they are carrying luggage, can only reach the airport on foot. Same goes for those who are there to receive some imminently arriving relative. Since they can't do this, they have to wait behind the barriers until the security measures are lifted and access to the airport is granted. Continuing on foot until they're inside, they won't be able to move into the respective departure lounges. They'll have to wait in the airport's main hall, or stay put until they're authorised to enter the café provided. The areas that allow access to the runway are strictly off-limits. The luggage can't be dispatched until there is a general announcement giving express authorisation to this effect. Gathering is forbidden: not in front of the check-in counters and not anywhere else.

At the 19 July 1976 meeting of the new leadership (Merbilhá, Mattini, Gorriarán), the Turk brought along the maps of the tunnels of the Maldonado stream. The Maldonado traverses the city of Buenos Aires, beneath the Avenida Juan B. Justo. It flows into the Río de la Plata, crossing the Jorge Newbery Airport at right angles. They laid out these plans on top of a well-lit table and discussed them at length.

At the point where it crosses the city of Buenos Aires's Jorge Newbery Airport, the Maldonado reaches a depth of two and a half metres.

The tunnel containing it, completed between 1929 and 1933, measures on this stretch about five and half metres in height.

These measurements, of course, are averages. Both the depth of the water and its distance to the tunnel's ceiling can vary, according to variations in the stream's normal volume, depending on incidental climatic factors.

In the month of September 1976, the reconnaissance of the Maldonado began.

In all, it was necessary to go down ten or twelve times. On the first of these, they went down at Floresta. Floresta is a distant, pleasant neighbourhood; almost on the opposite side of the city relative to the location of the Jorge Newbery Airport.

In the uniform, regular layout of the city of Buenos Aires, in the well-known monotony imposed upon it by the grid, the Maldonado, and hence the avenue covering it, stands out in an unexpected diagonal, a short cut and a zigzagging, a rare plasticity, an alteration that is all too obvious.

The Avenida Juan B. Justo bears the name of the founder of the Socialist Party in Argentina. He was the first translator into Spanish of Karl Marx's *Das Kapital*.

The Jorge Newbery Airport bears the name of the heroic pioneer of aeronautics in Argentina. He met his death, as if by fate, in an aviation accident.

They went down into the Maldonado using the storm drains. They lifted the black cast-iron covers and got in that way.

They hid themselves, when they could, dropping down from the rear compartment of the van, through the hole that had been made for this purpose in roughly the middle of the floor and loosely covered with a piece of metal sheeting. But it wasn't always possible to do this.

They'd go down first thing in the morning, when there was almost nobody on the streets. The tasks they needed to do down below could take them several hours. In any case, they'd come back up without fail before the night drew in, because that sort of behaviour, in the darkness, if they were detected, could only be suspicious.

During the day, they took great trouble not to be seen. If they were, however, they could perfectly well pass for a work crew, carrying out maintenance tasks or even doing cleaning work on the Maldonado.

The Benito Urteaga special unit bears the name of the man who fell in an armed confrontation, together with Roberto Mario Santucho, whose number two he was, in an apartment at 3149 Calle Venezuela, Villa Martelli, on 19 July, 1976.

Further west, in the more distant neighbourhoods, the points of entry, or of descent, into the tunnels of the Maldonado were more accessible. This was necessary, because, after a first reconnaissance mission, they decided to make use of a rubber dinghy for moving around down below and transporting the various tools.

What they needed to transport, altogether, weighed about a hundred and twenty kilos.

They managed to get hold of the boat. They lowered it into the tunnel. They left it tied firmly to a brick crossbeam, in a marked location.

They assembled a good set of exploratory gear including, for example, submersible flashlights, strong ropes, waterproof wrapping material.

They began their operations out of Floresta. From then onwards, in successive trips, they moved closer: Avenida Córdoba, the Puente Pacífico area, and onward, till they reached the Jorge Newbery Airport.

In Floresta the streets are more desolate, often they're completely empty, people are more inclined to stay home (if they do go out, it's only around mid-morning, and just to do a bit of shopping, that's all. After that, they come back. Since they are acquainted with each other, if they run into each other, they might stop to chat on a corner, shopping bags on the ground, hands in their pockets or on their waists, or arms crossed in front of their bodies).

There was less danger of being seen, in this area, with fewer passers-by, less traffic.

But there was, at the same time, a greater risk of attracting people's attention. These neighbourhoods are more stable, more homogenous, more routine, more like themselves from one day to the next. Anything different that happens, any change to the rhythm of the landscape, has got to be noticed: it attracts people's eyes like a flicker of light, a flash.

One thing makes up for the other. The flatness of the everyday ends up prevailing.

That was where they lowered the rubber dinghy, after identifying an entranceway that was more generous.

They did it very early on a Sunday. Maintenance work, activities for preventing blockages, aren't affected by time off, by non-working days. That would be their cover.

At that time of that day, however, there was almost nobody on the streets of Floresta. It was as if the city had been evacuated. Or subjected (as indeed it was) to the strictures of a curfew. One might have believed it deserted: the places intact, but void of any people. Or one might have believed it in obedience to a general confinement order. People were there, but inside. Not going out and not looking out and never knowing.

They acted with the greatest discretion, and with practised alacrity.

Soon the boat was down below: resting on the Maldonado.

They arrived unseen.

They left unnoticed.

Then they carried down the charge. About two hundred kilos of dynamite.

For this, they did use the opening in the floor of the back of the Citroneta.

They went down in secret and they came up in secret: invisible.

They happened to find a storm drain that offered them the possibility of parking immediately above it, without the van sticking out too much into the middle of the street, which would have seemed strange.

The Citroneta's metal plating was thin, pierceable.

They slipped through that hole, the one in the floor of the van, then immediately through a second hole, the one in the street, the one in the city.

They left the explosives in the rubber boat.

And the rubber boat tied with a rope on a bend in the tunnels of the stream, in the bowels, so to speak, of Buenos Aires.

The first step, the riskiest, had now been taken.

If they were to be intercepted, driving around in the Citroneta or during their descent manoeuvres, the worst would be for this to happen while they were transporting the explosives. In such circumstances, they couldn't have forged their alibi of the municipal team, of sewer maintenance, nothing of the kind.

Now the explosives were down below.

What would follow was the underground journey, to transport everything gradually towards the airfield zone.

They had to do it by day. Go down by day and come up by day.

One of them, it could have been Martín, once mentioned the old mole.

The others celebrated the idea.

It was quite relevant, this figure that Marx had taken from Shakespeare, no less. But to them, the figure was no longer a mere figure. To them, it seemed to have become literal. They were the real old mole.

Digging beneath the ground, advancing without being seen, plotting tunnels in secret; waiting for the moment when they would emerge, bursting out.

The waters of the Maldonado were clouded, foul-smelling.

The stream, in itself, must have been pretty filthy. To that, one would now have to add the vile discharge of waste.

The tunnels were in darkness practically the whole way. From time to time, through some peephole, a pale parody of light would come in from the surface. It never lasted long. Very soon the darkness would return.

Their progress was slow, the boat's journey laboured.

What didn't occur to anyone, however, was the obvious idea of the descent into hell. That was impossible. Hell was up above.

They needed to protect the explosives from the damp of the stream itself. For this, they kept them wrapped in synthetic coverings.

The cables they were transporting couldn't be allowed to get wet either.

The boat withstood everything, but it was already completely imbued with the foul air of the tunnel.

Above them, the neighbourhoods followed one another.

Floresta, Villa Santa Rita, La Paternal.

Then would come Villa Crespo. Then, Palermo.

Then the forest area.

Then the airport.

There was one day when everything became dangerous, or seemed to.

They had worked a lot and well on the transporting of the materials. They had made a fair bit of progress, loading up and rowing.

They were satisfied, but exhausted.

As planned, they emerged through a storm drain close to Avenida Córdoba.

The van, in this instance, could not be parked exactly there, it would have seemed inappropriate. It was waiting to one side, up against the pavement.

They needed to push the heavy black cover from below, move it aside, climb upward and out onto the road as swiftly as possible (though without any haste: haste is something people notice). Then return the cover to its position, arrange it with a couple of moves, stroll away from the space absolutely normally, get into the Citroneta, leave.

That was what they needed to do and that was what they did.

But at the very moment of peering out and emerging, they encountered a passer-by who, on one of the adjacent pavements, stopped to watch them. Not that he was walking and looked at them; that's something that happened every day. Not that he was walking and looked at them; he stopped to watch.

Something about them, or about the scene, seemed to him, suddenly, inappropriate.

All these movements blend in, as a rule, with the whole shapeless mass of things that happen in the vast city. Things happen all the time, and nobody registers any of them. An inertia of normality absorbs them and dissolves them. It's assumed that each thing that happens, happens for some reason; and that for some purpose, everything that is done is done.

Nobody notices, nobody asks.

And yet, this time, as they climbed up and appeared, they encountered this guy. Who was just walking along the pavement and stopped. He stopped because he saw them, he stopped to look at them. And since he had stopped, that's how he remained: looking at them.

Very likely he wasn't thinking about anything. Not anything concrete, no concrete suspicion. A kind of hunch, at all events. A squeak in perception that intimated to him that something was happening.

For a second, being looked at, they stopped still. Which was a complete mistake. Being still was the same thing as acknowledging discovery. It lasted a second and that second passed. They resumed what they were doing. They proceeded naturally, with an air of routine. What would a team do who'd just repaired a flaw in a junction box or cleared the mud from an air vent or tipped disinfectant liquids along the culverted stream? They would do no more nor less than everything they were doing.

The guy, notwithstanding this, went on looking.

Was it simple bored curiosity or did he suspect something? Was he just a local or somebody who could get them into trouble? Would he go on watching a little while longer, just watching, an incidental witness, or was he inclined to tell?

Doubts hovered about the scene while they, as if nothing was up, finished climbing out of the tunnel, cleaned themselves off and straightened out their clothes, replaced the cast iron cover onto the storm-drain hole in the street and started to walk, their steps calculatedly unhurried, towards the idle van.

Until the guy seemed to decide for himself, that, no, nothing was happening.

He decided nothing was happening and he went.

And as he went, he did indeed decide that, no, nothing was going to happen.

They saw him move away down Córdoba. As he moved away, he gradually lost importance.

Slowly they boarded the Citroneta. They started it up. And then they moved away, too.

But in the opposite direction.

This very specific instant of anxiety, overcome just like that, produced in each of them an effect of invulnerability. They gained in confidence. They felt less exposed and not more. There was no doubt that they would reach the airport without being discovered. They would carry out the operation. They would succeed in shaking up the board.

It was not this incident, however, the one with the busybody, that was the greatest danger they encountered, but another, much worse, which almost put an end to everything (and to everyone).

They had reached Palermo. More precisely, they were around Puente Pacífico.

In this sector of the city, the tunnel enclosing the Maldonado must be added to others, some adjacent ones, those from the D-line of the underground railway, a branch that ended (or began) its route precisely here.

The sounds in this place were different.

Perhaps it was the subway, or perhaps the trains that run above it across an iron bridge, that added vibrations that they had previously ignored. All this meant they felt less isolated than in other parts: more connected to the outside world and to the implied normal life of the city.

And besides, they were very aware that, just across the Avenida Santa Fe, diagonally to the subway openings and parallel to the San Martín train tracks, was the barracks of the Regiment of Patricians. They had it, so to speak, right above them: its troops, its barracks, its arsenal.

There they were, hard at their work, resolutely transporting their heavy cargo, when up above, on the outside, in the city, it suddenly began to rain.

An unexpected rain, unforeseen, unannounced, incompatible with the discreetly clouded sky they'd had in sight only a short while earlier.

They heard it, or thought they heard it. The water outside was intensifying.

The rain, being unexpected, seemed to need to be furious, too. Falling from one moment to the next and falling all at once.

The streets get waterlogged when that happens. The drains insufficient. The water covers, first of all, the road surface and then starts rising, without let-up, to the kerbs, towards the pavements.

In Buenos Aires, nobody is unaware of this, there are certain neighbourhoods that always flood.

They flood (La Boca, Barracas, the Avenida Juan B. Justo and environs) not only from the water falling from above, but also, and especially, from the water brimming up from below.

And indeed: the stream did begin to grow.

Gradually, but incessantly. And above all: uncommonly fast.

The volume of water was on the increase, as if someplace somebody were opening one sluice after another, discharging a whole sea through this precarious tube, which looks suddenly narrow.

The Maldonado was rising without cease. But every once in a while it seemed to receive, not just a continuous addition, but deluges of water in dizzying bursts: water in punches or thrusts, desperate water, under pressure.

The course of the stream was turning into a torrent.

They secured the boat with ropes, so as not to be swept away.

But the greatest danger was not the force of the water, but rather the way in which, as it grew, it was rising.

The boat itself, and they in the boat, were getting ever closer to the ceiling. Soon there would be no space at all. The stream would occupy the whole thing.

First of all, they needed to get their cargo to safety.

They wrapped up the explosives, until they were watertight, cramming them into a generous hollow formed at an irregular angle by a pillar and a girder.

Now they needed to get out themselves.

It didn't look easy.

They'd have to move against the current, because they knew the exits they could rely on upstream. Downstream they didn't know. That way lay the forests. Maybe there wouldn't be any.

The water was flowing hard. But more than that, it was rising. Already they had barely any room. The boat was beginning to be squeezed between the Maldonado and the ceiling. The air was starting to run short.

The oars were not enough. They used the ropes. One of the group would get into the water, swim with rope in hand till he had reached some firm spot, and tied the rope there. Then they'd have to pull on the rope and make their progress that way: an ascent.

It was a little like scaling a cliff. But horizontally.

They applied this method several times. It worked.

But the water didn't stop rising, because up above, it didn't stop raining.

They had to duck down in the boat. Their heads were already almost touching the ceiling. They might knock into the girders.

A badly-tied rope came loose at one point, and they lost several metres they'd managed to progress.

But at the same time, they realised that the ceiling and the girders which were so close, which were what threatened them, could also be of some help.

There was barely any space for rowing now.

The movement was the opposite of a collapse, but the effect was the same: crushing.

Except that the ceiling and the girders, being so close, could also be used to secure themselves and to push themselves off.

Oars to one side.

The rope ahead, and pulling.

And at the same time, inside the boat, face up, pressing palms against the ceiling, driving fingers into the girders and all in unison propelling themselves in the opposite direction to that of the Maldonado stream.

There was already water in the boat and they were sheltered, squashed, in that thin remnant between the water and the concrete.

Until they finally arrived, panting, at a generously wide drain.

It wasn't far above them: it was right there.

They pushed and managed to shift it. They'd be able to get out.

But first, they needed to secure the boat. They mustn't lose the boat, mustn't let the water drag it away.

They tied it, restrained it, tightened it, reinforced it. And they came out.

The flood meanwhile had emptied the streets.

They were back on Avenida Córdoba.

The rain, though heavy, seemed to them, by contrast,

rather inoffensive. The same water, but fragmented. It got in the mouth, certainly. But it wasn't enough to suffocate.

The great relief made them feel happy. Saved, and therefore whole.

Indeed, a few minutes later, now in the Citroneta, everyone was in a state of sheer hysterics. They laughed without saying anything, and they couldn't stop.

It wouldn't be long. It really wouldn't be long now.

Another descent or two would be enough.

Another descent or two and they'd be at the airfield.

That is, level with the airfield. And, strictly speaking, under the airfield.

The Turk knew.

The airport runway was metre-thick extra-hard concrete.

In order to blow it up, they would need between nine and twelve kilos of TNT.

They would plant this, and they'd plant more.

Because it wasn't just a question of blowing up the runway.

What they wanted was for the explosion to reach the plane at the point of take-off.

Auntie knew, too.

They were all resolved.

It was not the same as reaching the shore, though one of them did make the joke and shouted 'Land!'

It wasn't the same as scrutinising the sky and its birds, as watching dark lines on the horizon, as deducing possible directions of currents or tides.

It was not the same as docking at port, it was not the same as mooring to the bank. They didn't need to drop anchor. They didn't need to climb onto the land.

But yes: they'd arrived.

The boat had held out. The explosives looked intact.

They had arrived. Where? Destiny.

The end of the journey.

The Jorge Newbery Airport.

The whole of this phase, of the boat journey in secret and in the dark, was over.

So now they moved to the next stage, that of the attack itself.

It was early November, 1976.

Since they could not plant a single charge, they used two.

A central load of thirty kilos of TNT and thirty-five kilos of Gelamon under the middle part of the runway.

And a second batch on the edge: fifteen kilos of TNT and fifty kilos of Gelamon.

The two charges connected in parallel to a main electrical power line, each of them with three triggers and several boosters.

Tied with robust cords to the Maldonado's ceilings. A good distance from the water and protected from the effects of the damp with an insulating wrapper.

Remote-control triggers weren't an option.

This area, like any airport, was saturated with radio and electrical interferences.

They couldn't run the risk of an accidental activation.

As a trigger, they used a long line of damp-proof cables, connected to a high-voltage energy source positioned at some distance.

They set it up. Got it all ready.

And now came the hardest part.

The hardest part?

Yes, the hardest part. Now they needed to wait.

They had already been bold.

They had already been daring.

They had already been surreptitious.

They had already been intrepid, rigorous, persistent.

Now they needed to be patient.

The charges had been planted right beneath the airport runway.

Now they needed to wait for the announcement of a flight into the interior by Jorge Videla. Some domestic flight, one of those ones that always take off from Jorge Newbery Airport.

The days in that country passed so dark and criminal, so fierce and so grim, so fearful and so murderous, that they did nothing but ratify their conviction, from that same July meeting, that a blow must urgently be struck against the regime: to shake up, once and for all, the board, and the course of history.

The official announcement came at last.

On Friday 18 February, 1977, the nation's president, Lieutenant General Don Jorge Rafael Videla, would depart in the morning, bound for the city of Bahía Blanca, in the province of Buenos Aires, where he would be fêted by the local authorities and take part in various meetings on matters of regional and national interest.

The day comes. It's here.

It is now 18 February. It's Friday. Seven a.m.

From the apartment on Calle Austria, the three of them leave: Pepe, David and Martín (that's what they're called now). They get into the Citroneta. They start it up and leave. They are headed for the Palermo park.

It's the three of them. They make up the Benito Urteaga squad of the People's Revolutionary Army, the armed wing of the Workers' Revolutionary Party.

These three men are responsible for this operation: Operation Seagull.

The action as a whole, though, involves some ten men in total. Auntie is accompanied by a second-in-command, in case something happens and he needs substituting at the moment of the crucial act. There are other guerrillas in the area, to perform containment tasks. And a few drivers arranged at certain strategic positions, to guarantee them an escape once the action has been completed, when the forces of repression react like ants in a kicked anthill: frantic, blind, desperate, lost.

David gets out at the Velodrome, in the Palermo park. The road at this point makes a zigzag: a curve and a countercurve. And it passes beneath two bridges, two railway bridges. It's easy to hide there, to remain alert and concealed.

There are no pavements on this stretch, nor anywhere to park.

Auntie, lieutenant Martín, also stations himself in the Palermo park; but in a different zone: closer to the Planetarium.

In the afternoons on any weekend, and especially now that it's summer, the place is filled with kids: they come to throw food to the ducks that wander around the artificial lake, they come to the Planetarium to discover what the universe is about: how it began, what it consists of.

At this time, so early on a Friday morning, the place is deserted.

Auntie takes up his position.

It is he who will press the button.

Pepe heads on towards the airport.

He leaves the van at an agreed spot, at a more than prudent distance, and continues on foot. He already knows that access is barred to traffic.

You would assume he's just here to fetch a relative who's coming in on some domestic flight.

The general notice that all of this morning's regular flights will suffer some delays has no reason to worry him, as indeed it does not. He has the time.

The people who are due to travel are waiting in the access areas.

Those who have come to fetch somebody arriving can wait in the café on the first floor of the Jorge Newbery Airport. They may not go out onto the terrace, it's forbidden. The doors are locked.

But they can peer through these doors or through the windows, and look out. Looking out and seeing: the open sky, the even course of the morning, the airport's runway, things happening.

8:10 a.m. Everyone is in place.

They communicate through remote transmitters, also called walkie-talkies.

They are using an uncommon frequency, to be sure they won't be intercepted.

Pepe, in particular, who of everyone is the most exposed, uses it with the greatest discretion: so that nobody notices when he presses a button, so that it looks, like with mad people, that he is muttering things to himself.

At 8:15 a.m., on the dot, the electrical source is connected to the trigger circuit.

It will be activated from the Palermo park, in the area round the Planetarium.

The runway of the Jorge Newbery Airport will be blown up.

At 8:30 a.m., a Fokker F28, Tango 02, starts to move.

On the plane, among others, is Videla.

From the airport, the notification comes in. First signal: plane on the move.

The notification is received, in the Palermo park, by the man responsible for triggering the detonation.

8:35. Second notification sent from the airport. The airplane is moving towards the northern head of the runway. It will take off from north to south.

Perfect. It's as expected.

The electrical lock is taken off the power source.

8:36. Tango 02, the Fokker on which Videla is travelling, is already at the northern end of the runway.

Taxiing will begin.

Pepe is watching everything at the airport. He's the one sending the notifications.

Lieutenant Martín receives them and he is ready to activate the trigger.

David is waiting in a supporting position.

It's 8:40.

The plane positions itself at the head of the runway. It stops.

It remains there a few seconds: motionless, pointing.

It gives the impression that it's assessing something, weighing something up: the runway, the sky, the trip itself.

As if it needed to take a moment before making its decision.

That's the impression it gives.

They, on the other hand, the Benito Urteaga special unit, are perfectly resolved. Pepe with his radio in hand, held up to his mouth. Martín in the park, listening out carefully, finger on the switch. The charge under the runway. Everything about them is decisiveness.

The plane, as if waking, begins to move.

It is still 8:40. Time had been suspended.

Pepe gives the notification: now.

The plane is already taxiing.

Martín in the park: presses the button. The trigger activates the battery. It detonates the charge. The explosion happens.

From below, from within, the runway explodes.

It flies up, in pieces. There is fire and noise. There's a shockwave. It reaches the plane.

The side charge was detonated. The one placed eight metres from the runway. It exploded furiously and surged upward with its blast, its aggression.

But the other explosive device, the one positioned level with the middle of the runway, didn't detonate.

Something went wrong, nobody knows what, and it didn't detonate.

The second charge didn't explode and nobody knows why.

No one knows why, or ever will.

But one charge does explode. It works and it explodes. It tears the runway up by the root, hurling a huge shuddering of shards at Videla's plane.

The detonation occurs eight metres from the runway.

And it catches the plane already taking off, fifteen metres up.

Because the plane, apparently, took off a little sooner than usual.

It took off a bit sooner, a bit further back.

Probably just because, because one take-off is never identical to another, because there are things that are pure chance, because luck always plays its part, too.

One charge did not explode and the plane took flight a little sooner.

The charge that does explode catches it in the air, at an altitude of fifteen metres.

It receives the shockwave further away than anticipated.

The explosion, however, does reach it.

The scattered shards strike a third of the fuselage.

The aircraft flounders, but keeps going.

It trembles, shudders, registers the blow.

But it doesn't plummet to the ground, or explode, or catch fire.

It trembles, shudders, registers the blow.

But it does take flight, despite everything.

A bird scared by the noise, by the injury. It gives a squeal of its engines then escapes, as best it can, into the sky. Wounded and in haste. It flees, upward. It transforms from a plane into a black line, a dark scratch across the sky. It transforms from a plane into a dot, a dot that's ever harder to make out. It transforms from a dot into nothing.

Taking with it the tyrant, unharmed.

It takes him out of danger, to get him out of danger.

Tango 02, which was transporting, among other very high-level officials, the nation's president, Lieutenant General Don Jorge Rafael Videla, bound for the city of Bahía Blanca, had to make an emergency landing, for preventative reasons, at Morón airport, to the west of the city of Buenos Aires.

In the Jorge Newbery Airport, an aimless urgency overtakes everything at once.

Shouting, a lot of shouting. And running all about.

Shouting. There are those who shout from the shock and those who shout orders. There are those who give information at the tops of their lungs: 'A terrorist attack!' And those who shout their disbelief: 'A terrorist attack?' Shouting, shouting, so many shouts, which overlap and fail to understand each other.

And running all about. Those who run to provide assistance (but to whom?): police officers, medical staff, plainclothes officers. They ask to get through, make their way through, and run, and run. Others run by instinct: to go, to escape. They run into one another. Not to mention the one who falls onto the floor, his things scatter.

'Did they kill Videla?'

'No. No, they didn't.'

The sound of sirens. Long, desperate howls, both outside and inside. Outside: squad cars launching themselves at full speed, to sweep the area, to clear it. Inside: the firemen's truck moves swiftly across the runway, arrives to stifle the modest fire that is still glowing. At the risk of there being another bomb. Because that's what a few people all around are saying. 'They've planted a bomb.' And a fear that there's another. Nobody really knows what to do. Or what to say. 'They've planted a bomb.' 'Apparently they've planted a bomb.'

'Did they kill Videla?'

'No. No, they didn't.'

In the general disorder, in the mad mixture of shouting and running, only one thing is gradually becoming defined with any clarity: the airport must be evacuated. This seems to unite the security forces, eager to re-establish order and take control of the situation, and those who just want to get away from the place as soon as they can.

Which is why it's easy, for Pepe, to slip away and get himself out.

On the street, the squad cars and the police motorbikes race past each other amid the clamour; soldiers with rifles leap from the vans; police officers come and go, very jumpy, their guns drawn. A few, in plainclothes, look threatening. 'Out, out!' they curse the confused bystanders who, being outside already, can't understand what it is they're supposed to do.

The stampede to the street stretched out like a trail of terrors, of worries. Each person has some view on how far they need to run: where the prudent distance begins, the distance that helps them feel like they're out of danger. There they can stop running and continue at a brisk walk. Or even stop and catch their breath a little, recover their calm.

Those fleeing in terror, because they were inside the airport, start to run into those who weren't in the place at all, those who were simply going about their normal lives. Cleaners for the waterfront food carts, administrators on their way to the university campus, some group of bus drivers just killing time at the head of the runway, a fisherman who started early this morning. 'What's happened? What's happened?' 'They've planted a bomb.'

Pepe walks quickly, but at no point does he run.

'Did they kill Videla?'

'No. Apparently not.'

He reaches the Citroneta. It is simple, slim, so like itself, so sober, filling him with absolute equilibrium, helping him to climb in and drive and leave the area without arousing anybody's suspicions.

The others manage to get away, too, without any trouble.

The support vehicles show up, as planned, at the pre-established locations.

All they need to do is get in and leave. And, not long after leaving the Palermo park behind them (the Velodrome, the Planetarium, the groves, the artificial lakes), mingle in with the other people, lose themselves in the general movement.

The news media bring some calm to the populace.

They notify them that, yes, there has indeed been

an attack by Marxist terrorists on the Jorge Newbery Airport: an explosive attack on the life of the nation's president.

But that the subversive attack failed and the nation's president is in perfect physical and mental condition. Waiting for the arrival of a new plane, which will allow him to resume his activities for the day exactly as they had been planned.

Only Pepe returns, with the van, to the apartment on Calle Austria.

In a while, Érica will get back from work.

They will talk about what happened and continue, until further orders, with their show of life as a couple.

There will be no contact with Auntie and David for a few days.

Each of those two has been taken to a different house, neither of them their own.

The radio stations repeat the information over and over.

The evening newspapers will already be sharing photographic images: a hazy view, in black and white, of the broken runway, with rubble; patches of grass and bits of the runway scattered across the runway itself and a hole that bears witness that an explosion took place there.

On 18 February, the People's Revolutionary Army publishes its 'military communiqué'.

It claims responsibility for the attack and points out that, despite having failed in its objective, it has proved that the regime is not invulnerable: that it's necessary to struggle against tyranny and that it can be defeated.

In April of that year, days after Operation Seagull, Pepe manages to get out of the country. He goes into exile.

In that same month of April, by the same route, the Turk also leaves the country, and goes into exile.

Lieutenant Martín's real name is Eduardo Miguel Streger. They called him Auntie, too, but his name was Eduardo Miguel Streger.

He was kidnapped on 12 May, 1977.

Statements from surviving witnesses suggest that he was taken to the secret detention centre called La Perla, in Córdoba province.

After that, he was never heard from again.

From that day, Friday 18 February, the domestic flights scheduled to run from the Jorge Newbery Airport started to operate instead from Ezeiza International Airport, in the city's outskirts.

Meanwhile General Videla carried out his visit to the General Mosconi platform, to the south of Bahía Blanca, where he was briefed on oil drilling in the Argentine Sea. There he ratified the national government's decision to intensify the exploitation of the country's natural resources, and announced to the press: 'The exploitation of energy sources will be accelerated.'

He returned to the capital that same day, with no further incidents being reported.

III

PLAZA MAYOR

'I'll pass,' says my grandmother.

I've just called envido. She pinches the tips of the playing cards, she peers at them again (she'd just done this), she shakes her head, rejecting it. Then I, after a pause, play a three of swords. She looks at it (looks at the three, looks at the swords) and plays a five of clubs. She presses it onto the table and pushes it forward, so that it ends up beneath my card.

I then play a ten: a ten of coins. And she puts a twelve on top of that: a twelve of clubs. She looks at me, expressionless.

'Truco,' she says.

I look at my card, though I know what it is. It's the seven of coins.

'I'm in,' I say.

She plays the seven of swords. She's beaten me. She knows she's beaten me. And she smiles.

'Who's keeping score?', I ask.

She shrugs.

'You do it,' she says.

I take a blue biro from my rucksack, tear a page out of a notebook. I divide it in two; on one side, an *a*, for *abuela* (my grandmother), on the other, a *y*, for *yo* (me, her grandson). Two little lines for my grandmother, one for me.

It's my turn to shuffle.

While I shuffle, she chats away. She draws subjects out of nothing. She talks about distant pasts, but as though they were close to us.

I never liked those friends of your dad's, she says. Oh, the high school ones I did, yes, they were good kids. But not the ones from college. I didn't like them, she says. I didn't like them.

I deal the cards. My grandmother receives hers, arranges them, part-opens them slowly, more to spy on them than to look at them. She plays a ten of coins.

'Envido,' I say.

'I'll pass,' she says.

I beat the ten with an eleven of clubs. I pause. I say nothing. I play an ace of coins.

'Piece-of-shit cards,' says my grandmother.

She quits. I jot down two lines for myself. A shape like a football goal has formed in my column. I push the deck towards my grandmother. Her turn to shuffle.

And the fact he went into Law, she says. I had my own prejudices: Philosophy, Psychology, Sociology. He chose Law and that sounded good to me. To your grandfather, too, as best I can remember. But your grandfather wasn't one for really set ideas. I was always the stronger character.

I love the way she shuffles. I do it more clumsily, joining and intermixing the two halves of the pack kind of by force. Whereas with her, it's like she makes the cards fly, like she makes them float between her hands. She does it the way magicians do it. And she doesn't need to look while she does it (I do).

She deals incredibly fast. The cards travel across the table unseen. I only see them when they reach my hands. I receive them, look them over.

'Envido,' I say.

'I'm in,' she says.

'Twenty-seven,' I say.

'Twenty-eight,' she says.

She smiles.

'These are better,' she adds.

I play a two of coins. She plays a two of cups. We're even.

Without a word, I play another two. The two of swords.

'Truco,' she says.

I look at her. I get the sense she's lying. My card's low, but I get the sense she's lying.

'I'm in,' I say.

She plays the ace of clubs. She was not lying.

It's four points to her. I make a note. Her square is fortified with the diagonal, plus one line more. Now I'm shuffling.

My grandmother starts up again. I took it for granted, she says, that over in Law there'd be a better sort. And it's not that I wasn't right. Only that your dad managed to get together with the very worst.

I ask her, while she cuts, while I deal, what that very worst refers to.

She makes a quick gesture, of not hearing or not understanding.

'Like hippies?' I specify. 'Sex, drugs? Counterculture?'

My grandmother scowls, as if in contempt. What are you on about, she says. Hippies indeed! Sex, drugs? On the contrary. Counterculture, you say? Don't even know what that is. If only they had been hippies, she says; hippies don't screw with anybody.

She picks up the cards, fans them out slowly. She smiles.

'Flor!' she announces.

'We never said if we were playing with flor.'

'Didn't we? Well, we're saying it now: flor!'

She says it and plays the strong seven. I go low: five of cups. She plays a four of swords. I beat it with the ten of coins. I wait.

'Truco,' I say.

'I'm in,' she says.

I play the seven of coins. And her? She doesn't flinch.

125

'Retruco,' she says.

Could she have the ace of swords? If she has any other card, she'll lose to me and she'll have been bluffing. But could she have the ace of swords?

'I'm in,' I say.

She plays it. It's the ace of swords.

Six points to her.

'How are we doing?' she asks.

'Twelve-three,' I answer.

'To who?' she asks.

I look at her.

'To you.'

She nods and shuffles. She speaks.

Hippies indeed! Long hair, long necklaces, all frocks and no hygiene. They lived on top of one another and that was all. But not this, this was different. In Psychology, fine. In Psychology, that's all there was. But in Law? In Law? Your father found them out. And befriended them. There was one, Marcelo, oh I didn't like him one bit. I didn't like any of them one bit. But Marcelo least of the least.

I look at my hand. I look at my grandmother.

'Envido,' I say.

'I'm in.'

'Twenty-eight.'

She grimaces.

'It's yours.'

I play the two of coins. She plays a seven of clubs.

'Go on, then, play the six of coins,' she says.

I do it. I play the six of coins. She beats it with an eleven of clubs. She stops to think a moment. She plays without a word. An ace of cups.

I've got a twelve. The twelve of swords. I lose.

'Truco,' I say.

'I'll pass,' she says.

I return my card to the pack, and record three points for myself. I start shuffling.

I told your grandfather, she says: that boy Marcelo, I told him. I don't like him one bit. I don't like our Angelito mixing with him so much. He's going to get him into some weird business. But your grandfather, who was such a good man, his character was weak. Life quite passed him by! Leave him be, he would say. Ángel is no child. He knows what he's doing. Oh, he knows what he's doing?, I'd ask. No, no, he doesn't.

I deal. My grandmother checks out her cards.

She plays a three of coins.

'Flor,' I say.

'Flor?' she says. 'We're playing with Flor?'

I beat her three of coins with the ace of clubs. I play the twelve of clubs. She beats it with the ace of cups.

'Truco,' she says.

'I'm in,' I say.

She plays the three of swords.

'Retruco,' I say.

'I'm in,' she says.

I play the three of clubs.

'First one to me,' I say.

'Yes, I do know that,' she says. 'You think I can't see?'

I jot down six points for myself. We're even. She shuffles the cards faster than before, but with the same perfection. The cards rain down on themselves, they touch and combine without colliding.

Your dad was already living with your mum. Always such a delight of a girl. But oh, yes: extremely reserved. To this day, says my grandmother: extremely reserved. I know the two of them were already living together. Not properly married, as God would have it, but living together. I tried to worm it out of him: d'you still see that Marcelo? Who is he, what's he do, what's he up to? And those other pals, the pals who introduced him to Marcelo, who are they? What are they up to? Those meetings they have, what are they for? Because I knew they were having these meetings.

My grandmother deals the cards. My three, her three. Each of us looks at their hand, trying to give nothing away.

'Envido,' I say.

'I'm in,' she says.

'Twenty-seven,' I say.

She shakes her head.

'It's yours.'

I play the three of swords. She plays the eleven of cups.

'Truco,' I say.

'I'll pass,' she says.

I show her the twenty-seven from the envido, I add three lines to my column, I take the pack and set about shuffling.

'I'm already past the halfway mark,' I say.

'Oh, really?' she says.

And she tells me how she'd never been able to get a word out of my mother. Extremely reserved. Just like now. Marcelo's a very studious lad, she'd answer. And you couldn't get her to go beyond that. And the others? The others, also good people. They're all friends of Ángel's. I knew they were having meetings. But surely all friends meet up, granny, I argue. To listen to music, drink beer, have fun. Yes, I do know that, says my grandmother, or do you think you lot were the ones who invented all that? That's not what I'm talking about. I'm talking about meetings.

She cuts. I deal. She receives her cards. Looks. Plays.

'Envido,' she says.

'I'll pass,' I say.

She plays the ace of coins. I beat it with the two of cups.

'Truco,' I say.

'I'll pass,' she says.

She gathers up the cards.

'Piece-of-shit hand,' she says.

I agree.

Your father had moved to a rather modest apartment. Yes, a modest place, but with a telephone. And in those days, getting hold of a telephone was no joke, oh don't you believe it. If you didn't have one, you needed to put in a request for one and you could be waiting years. Your father over in Jonte, in the Jonte building, well, he really had nothing to spare. Your mother, thank God, never aspired to all that much. The bathroom couldn't have been more basic, the living room was the tiniest thing, no bigger than this: from here to that wheelchair, you might say; no more than that. But yes, enough to live. And besides, they had a telephone. You're a proper tycoon!, I used to say to him. Because in those days a phone wasn't something just anybody had at home. And he did. And yet, he was always dropping by and talking on the phone at ours. Sometimes more than once a day. He'd come over and scrounge the telephone. And hey, I'm not saying that to be stingy, you know. Don't go thinking that about your grandmother. Because the phone in those days wasn't even metered! The metering came later, with the companies. Not at that time: you talked as much as you wanted and always paid the same. But I did feel funny about it. Why would your father come over to speak on the phone at home? Because sometimes that's the impression he gave: that he was coming over to talk on the telephone. He'd give each of us a kiss, chat with me a little and with your grandfather a little more, and then he'd go straight to the telephone. And I'd think: this is what he's come for. The truth was, that was what he came for. And then I'd wonder: why does he come to talk here? Why doesn't he talk from his house?

From time to time my grandmother shuffles. From time to time she seems to get distracted, and forgets to shuffle.

One night I grabbed your grandfather, I grabbed your grandfather and I said: Anselmo, there's something fishy going on. But your grandfather was so naïve! A good man, I can't deny it, but so naïve! Our Angelito's mixed up in something strange, I said to him. Why does he come over to talk here?, I said. He must be mixed up in something strange, I said. Your grandfather burst out laughing. Just imagine: laughing! He started laughing and he answered: he must have some girl on the side… and he doesn't want Susana to find out. A girl on the side?, I said to him. There's no girl: he's much too dozy for things like that. Don't you read the papers? Don't you have any idea what's going on? He did know, he did, says my grandmother. But he just didn't think. They plant bombs, kidnap people, they raid barracks, they shoot each other!, I said. I said that to him, said my grandmother. And poor Anselmo, always so naïve, he answered: you watch too many movies.

My grandmother gives me the deck to cut. I cut. She deals the cards.

I mean, really, she says: such a foolish thing to say. His answer was so foolish. Movies? What movies was I watching? The afternoon soaps and that's it! Open your eyes, Anselmo, I said. Open your eyes. There's something fishy going on.

'Envido,' I say.

'I'll pass,' she says.

I play a twelve, the twelve of swords. She plays a two, the two of coins. And another two after that: the two of cups.

'Another crappy hand,' she says.

'Looks that way,' I say.

One point to her, one point to me. A line in the y column and a line in the a column.

'You're not halfway yet,' I say.

'Oh?' she says. 'And what do I care?'

She pushes the cards over to my side of the table, for me to shuffle. I shuffle.

I shuffle badly, worse than ever. A couple of cards fall out.

'Careful,' she says, 'don't bend them.'

I knew, from the papers, that there was phone tapping. I knew from the papers, not from the movies like your grandfather said. A good man, your grandfather, but so naïve. Life quite passed him by. I knew, and I knew it from the newspapers, that there was phone tapping. They could get onto your line and listen to the things you were saying. And if I knew it, me who wasn't exactly very savvy, you can be sure those friends of your father's knew it. To me it was obvious they were all tangled up in something strange (your grandad said they weren't). And I was scared, of course, that they would drag him off with them too. Roberto I didn't worry about. Cristina it didn't even occur to me. But your dad had ended up kind of like your grandfather: so good-natured, so obliging. That's what worried me. And then I'd say to your grandfather: so tell me, Anselmo, tell me this one thing, why does he come over to make phone calls from here? And him, always so naïve, he'd answer: and what do you care? I knew they preferred to call from public phones. And if not them, then some house that wasn't being 'marked' (my grandmother makes air-quotes with her fingers). But public phones, in those days, you can imagine: they hardly ever worked. And it wasn't easy to get hold of the tokens, if you didn't have any (because they worked with tokens, not with normal coins). But more than that, I suppose, you were always putting yourself at risk of someone hearing you. Because you were talking on the pavement, or in bars, or in pharmacies. And the other people who came to talk would stand in line right behind whoever was there already, and well, you can imagine, they'd hear everything. I thought that was why your father came to call from home. Because he'd talk ever so quietly. And he'd put his hand over the bottom part of the receiver. What did he think I was, deaf? Or that I was naïve like your grandfather? Poor Anselmo, the poor thing. Life quite passed him by.

I listen and keep on shuffling.

'Hey, listen,' says my grandmother, 'you're going to wear them out!'

I give them to her to cut. She cuts. I deal. When my grandmother deals, she does it by throwing each card like an envelope slipped under a door, like a lunge, a stab. I'm gentler, I'm more like passing them over to the other person. She waits till she's received all three to pick them up and see what luck has in store for her in each hand.

She plays a two of clubs.

'Flor,' I say.

'What?' she says.

'Flor!' I say.

'Oh,' she says. 'Well, they do seem to just keep falling right into your lap today, don't they? Still,' she adds, 'lucky at cards…'

And she laughs at her own joke.

'God knows why we're playing with flor anyway,' she remarks then. 'That's how people play when they don't know what this game is really about.'

'You're the one who said,' I say.

'Oh?' she says. 'Are you sure?'

I play another two. The two of cups. I put it almost

next to hers, barely on top of it, as if wanting to emphasise the similarity.

'Well look at that,' she says. 'You made a match.'

'Yes,' I say. 'I made a match.'

'Truco!' she says.

She says it with some emphasis. I think she's lying.

I haven't got much: a king of cups, an eleven of cups. I hoped to force her hand and it didn't work out. Still, I think she's lying. Now she looks at me, defiant; which makes me sure. She's lying: she's got nothing. But I haven't got anything either: a king, a knight. Not much.

'I'll pass,' I say.

'You chickened out,' she says.

I show the flor.

'You win with that,' she says and adds her cards to the pack.

I jot down the points. By now, I have already collected four squares with a diagonal line going down through them from left to right. My grandmother has three. We're twenty-fifteen.

She shuffles and talks. She tells me that she started to eavesdrop on the calls my dad made from her house. One thing caught her notice: she didn't know a single one of the people he named. How was that possible? She knew about Marcelo, the one she liked least. She'd seen him when Ángel was still living with them. A brat who was always explaining things, always making speeches. She knew Luisito, who'd done high school with Ángel and who'd also gone into Law. She knew Mónica, who'd been Ángel's sort-of girlfriend. Then they had a fight and then my dad met my mum who she, my grandmother, liked much more. There were others too she was aware of from having heard them mentioned: Beto, the Eyetie, Julio, Auntie, big Graciela, little Graciela, Enrique, Juan, Rubén. How was it possible, says my grandmother, that my father was arranging to meet up, gatherings of friends, seeing them at one person's house, or the other's house, taking this one over to that one, or that over to the other, and never naming a single one of them, naming only those she didn't know? Your grandfather, says my grandmother, insisted that I always expected to know everyone. Your grandfather, poor thing. And I'd say to him: no, no, Anselmo, can't you tell they're using fake names? Too much time at the movies, too many movies, your grandfather would say. Honestly: when the last thing I'd seen in the cinema had been back home watching the old reels with Libertad Lamarque in them, what cinema was this man even talking about? They had aliases, it was obvious. They were up to something strange. Well, you can learn things in the cinema, I told your grandfather. He laughed.

Our ways of handing over a deck to be cut are also very different. I hold the shuffled pack out close to my grandmother, like it was an offering, like an invitation. She bangs it down on the table sharply, as though by doing this she was killing a bug, or trying to give someone a fright, or cutting off a conversation.

We're different in handing over a deck to be cut and different in the cutting itself, too. I do it without paying any attention. I just grab a portion of the cards and separate them simply from the rest. My grandmother, meanwhile, seems to be calculating, weighing up, as if she had divinatory powers or X-ray vision, as if she could know how the cards are arranged in the pack and then chose, in the cut, which ones would appear and which wouldn't, which would come to me and which to her.

I play a three of coins.

'Envido,' she says.

'I'll pass,' I say.

She looks at me.

'Truco,' she says.

'I'll pass,' I say.

She drops the cards contemptuously onto the pack without playing.

'You pass on this, pass on that,' she grumbles. 'How am I supposed to play like this? It's always passing with you, always passing.'

I jot down her two points.

'You're past halfway,' I say.

'Really?' she says. 'Well, it was about time.'

'Sorry to interrupt, Señora Mirta,' one of the assistants of the home appears beside us. 'It's time for your meds.' She accompanies the announcement by placing an almost transparent plastic box onto the table; inside it, there are pills of all colours, divided up into little compartments. 'Just hang on a moment while I fetch your water.'

Around us, there's one who's fallen asleep and has been gradually tipping over in her chair, another who is eating a sort of cracker and scattering crumbs as she chews, another gazing into the distance as she babbles memories, another who's talking to one who isn't listening and another who's talking to one who is listening but doesn't answer her nor ever will. That's the prevailing air. Mounted on a black stand from which there are various cables dangling, there is a TV set, turned on, with the volume muted. They're showing a news bulletin. Deaths of varying types are announced: deaths in muggings, deaths in traffic accidents, celebrity deaths, deaths in natural disasters. The sounds are coming from elsewhere, coming from a medium-sized radio that they have on a shelf. It is old melodic music from the seventies. All the songs they play ring a bell, I might even know some of the lyrics, at least in the choruses; but I'm never able to identify who it is that's singing them, what songs they are exactly.

My grandmother seems a bit lost herself sometimes. Today's a very good day. On days like today, she doesn't fit in, speaking positively, with her surroundings. She gives no indication that she realises, as if she wasn't registering the others or as if in some way she knew, or at least sensed, that on less well-favoured days, she too might find herself like that, like the other women, and so it's best for her not to say anything. The assistant comes back and hands her a cup of water. 'Thank you, dear,' my grandmother says to her. The pills are passed from one to the other. There are five in total. With each one she's handed comes the corresponding specification: for your blood pressure, for your cholesterol, for your calcification, etc. As if my grandmother were evaluating, each time, depending on the particular case, whether she will agree to swallow it or whether she'll refuse (in reality, there's nothing like that going on: the assistant is giving the details mainly for my benefit). My grandmother swallows with short, mechanical sips, without throwing her head back, without emphasising any related movement. Then the assistant moves away, to continue with her regular round of chemical supplies. 'Nice girl,' says my grand-mother. 'Her name's Mary,' she adds. 'Mary?' 'Yes, Mary. I think so.'

For a moment we're not sure, neither she nor I, whose turn it is now to shuffle and deal. The pack was left in the middle.

'Whose turn is it?' I say.

'What for?' she says.

'To deal,' I say.

'Oh,' she says. 'I don't know. You, I think.'

I pick up the pack and start to shuffle. My grand-mother recaps. So I was telling you about that lad Marcelo, she says. About him and those other friends of your father's I didn't like one bit. Mixed up in something strange, no doubt about that. And if you'd asked me they were using your father. Taking advantage, I thought, of how he was such a good young man, so good and so generous. If you'd asked me they were using him, they'd got him working as a messenger. Since they would be, like I say, compromised, they'd ask Angelito (why did I ever call him Angelito!) to pass on communications. And he'd have agreed, generous like he was. And so that he wouldn't get himself into any problems, or your mother, he'd do like I'm telling you, says my grandmother: he'd come over to the house, let us have a bit of a chat, and then he'd ask for the telephone. And on the phone I'd hear him, I eavesdropped and listened, he'd give information for meetings, for meetings or get-togethers, station platforms or corners, such-and-such a house or some other, or he'd tell them how so-and-so was doing, or some other person, like somebody calling a distant relative to pass on the latest family bulletin. And to me, who knew his friends, on the whole, and several of his college classmates too, none of those names rang a bell, I didn't recognise any of them, and that caught my attention too.

She suddenly discovers the three cards next to her hand. She's a little surprised to see them. She picks them up and considers them with her eyebrows slightly arched. 'Let's see, let's see, let's see,' she says. And she runs over them gradually, separating them slightly from below.

'Envido,' she says.

I look at my hand. Twelve of clubs, seven of clubs, three of cups.

'I'm in,' I say.

'Twenty-eight,' she says.

I nod.

'It's yours,' I say.

She plays a two of swords. I beat it with the three.

I play the twelve. She beats it with an ace of coins. I surmise that the card she has left in her hand is a six of swords or a seven of coins. I'd win against the first. Not the second.

'Truco,' she says.

Now I get scared.

'I'll pass,' I say.

She shows me the card, I've got to see her twenty-eight. It's the six of swords. It was the six of swords.

'That's what you get for being chicken,' she says.

She laughs. I smile at her. I jot down the points.

'We're even,' I say. 'Twenty apiece.'

'Yes,' she says. 'I know.'

She shuffles. Not a lot, but well. She gives it to me to cut, and I cut. She deals the cards with a speed in her fingers that wouldn't have seemed possible just minutes ago when, one by one, she took her pills. With the cards already in her hands, but without having looked at them yet, she says: One day I laid a little trap for your father. And he, poor thing, walked right into it.

She spreads her cards, looks at them. Then I do the same. She gestures to the table, for me to play, indicating that it's my turn.

'Envido,' I say.

'Raise,' she says.

'I'm in.' I don't even think about it.

I pause.

'Thirty-two,' I say.

'To hell with it,' she says. 'It's yours.'

I play the siete bravo, the seven of swords. She plays low: four of clubs. I play my five of swords, she already knows I've got it, just keeping nice and quiet, taking it calm. She, slowly, places the seven of clubs on top of it.

'Truco,' she says.

I've got a three.

'I'm in,' I say.

Emphatic, categorical, happy, my grandmother plays the ace of swords.

'Take that!' she exclaims.

'Oh, okay then,' I say to her.

'Take that!' she says again.

I write down the points. Four to me, for the envido, and two to her, for the truco. Still, she's the one who's elated, not me. Playing her strongest card like that, as if thumping her fist down right in the middle of the table, has fired her up with a burst of euphoria.

I take up the cards, my turn to shuffle. But before I do it, I look at my grandmother and I say: you were telling me about a trap you set for my dad once. A trap?, she's puzzled. For your father? And me, so that she will resume her story: a trap, yeah, that's what you said. That you got him to walk right into it.

That expression, about walking right into it, seems to reconnect her, to return her to where she was.

Oh, yes, yes, she says. An innocent little trap, hardly anything at all. Your father never even noticed. Maybe that's why he walked right into it. Because I was sure that Marcelo, he's the one I liked least of all of them, had some trouble about him; as for him, yes, I was quite certain he was mixed up in things and I'd always been afraid he'd drag your father in. Then in the group there was Mónica too, there'd been a romance between them before, and there's always some bond left behind when that happens (that's why we've got that old saying about where there once was fire). And a couple of lads from college who your father especially liked. But his weakness, and it was a weakness, was Luisito. Him and Luisito had known each other practically since they were little kids. They'd become friends at school, you know, says my grandmother, when they were, what? Twelve, thirteen. They shared their time at school then went on into Law together. Then one afternoon, when your father had stopped by at home, and I was kind of distracted, just looking like this, kind of the other way, I said: 'Ah, such a waste about that Luisito, isn't it? Seemed like such a clever boy.' And your father got totally furious, he turned red and his mouth tightened, you remember how he used to get, well, no, you don't remember. Flushed with rage and trying to hold himself back, he stared hard at me and said 'Why a waste?' And me, as if I was hardly thinking about what I was saying, I went 'Oh, wasting his time with those pals of his, and such a good student he used to be.' Your father tried to ignore me, but he couldn't; or he could, but first he answered: 'Following your ideals is never a waste of time.' Then I knew Luisito was mixed up in this business too, and I got worried; and I said to myself that the sooner I got your father away from that circle, the better. At that point I calmed him down, I pacified him with nice words: 'You know I do love Luisito,' I must have said something like that. And he calmed down. But I'd got it into my head. If you'd asked me, they were using him: as a messenger, a connection. He was always such a good mediator, so good at bringing people together. They would've been using him for that. But I had to get him out of there.

It was around that time, says my grandmother, that I thought of talking to the colonel.

I have the pack of cards in my hand. But tight and still: motionless.

'Are you asleep or what?' she says. 'You've got to shuffle, you've got to shuffle the cards.'

So I start shuffling. But the cards feel softer in my hands, too flexible, as if they were damp, and I can't merge them well together. Or is it that I've got a bit of perspiration on my hands and I'm the one who's making the cards practically wet? Before my grandmother gets agitated and starts to express her usual card-player's impatience, I decide to change my shuffling technique. Instead of the movement in the air, with my hands doing the mixing, I divide the little heap into two and put the two parts, which are more or less two halves, facing one another, touching or almost touching. I run my thumbs down the sides, like somebody rifling through the pages of a book he isn't going to read, just having a look. And pressing the two little heaps closer together as I do so, I get the cards on one side to thread in between the cards on the other. Then I push the piles together and re-form the one single deck, straightening it against the table; and finally I repeat the operation: I divide up the two little heaps, make them face each other, run my thumbs down the sides, thread one half into the other, combine everything, tidy it, and hand it over to be cut.

My grandmother cuts with gestures that are precise, measured, as if to demonstrate, by contrast, what a song and dance I've made of it. I get ready to deal, but I stop, suspended, mid-gesture. Which colonel?, I say to my grandmother. She looks at me, intrigued. Which colonel what?, she says. It's like a word game. One of those games where each person has to repeat the phrase spoken by the other person, but adding, with each turn, one more word to the sentence. The colonel you thought about talking to, I say: who was he? I wasn't thinking about talking to him, she says. I did.

She gestures with her chin, telling me to deal. To just deal, once and for all.

I deal.

I want to do it swiftly, I want to do it smoothly. But it doesn't come out right, I can't do it: I can't get the cards (her three, my three) to fall onto one another, ready to be picked up. They first need to be collected together. And then, yes, and not without some suspense, look at what each of us has been landed with.

My hand: a ten of clubs, a five of cups, a six of coins. Absolutely nothing at all whatsoever. Not for a truco and not for an envido, the worst hand possible. My only chance of adding some points in this round is to lie. To lie, and for her to believe me. But I don't feel like lying right now. Or, in reality, I haven't got the confidence. I'm sure she'd find me out.

So I play without a word.

I play the ten.

'Envido,' she says.

'I'll pass,' I say.

She beats the ten with an eleven of swords.

'Truco,' she says.

'I'll pass,' I say.

She gathers up the cards with some impatience.

'What is this?', she says. 'Are we playing truco or chess?'

I put another two lines in her column. They complete a square.

'We're even,' I say.

She looks at me.

'What do you mean, even? So I'm not in the lead? But you're passing on everything!'

I show her the sheet of paper with the scores. The two columns: the *y* for *yo* and the *a* for *abuela*. In each one, four squares that are crossed by a diagonal line, going down from left to right, and a fifth square that's still clear. Both the same. Twenty-four to twenty-four.

'That's from all the flors you got yourself,' she says.

Another assistant at the home, who looks like the previous one, comes over to where we're sitting. 'I'm sorry, Doña Mirta,' she says to my grandmother, 'but you know it's seven already, we'll be giving you your food soon.' She addresses her, but she's talking to me. She's telling me, in her way, that I'll soon have to leave. Here in the nursing home, which isn't what anybody calls this place, there are no visiting hours the way there are in regular hospitals; but there are tolerable time slots and unacceptable ones, which are established according to common sense: lunch and dinner-times, sacrosanct siestas, night. Still, people coming to visit are always made welcome, not only by those they are visiting but also by the staff, and even by those witnesses to the scene who, however out of it they might be, however absent they might be, still seem to celebrate what's happening, so that ultimately schedules become elastic and exceptions abound. Those people who come in from outside seem to revitalise those who are in here (even those who, like the staff, can in fact leave).

My grandmother introduces me: 'My grandson.' And she adds: 'Tell me, dear: your name's slipped my memory.' 'Susy,' says Susy. With that, my grandmother already considers her introduced. She questions her: 'And what are they giving us for dinner?' Susy answers: 'Chicken and mash.' My grandmother persists: 'Leg or breast?' Susy is straight-forward: 'Breast.' My grandmother goes on the attack: 'And are they going to throw a bit of salt into my food, this time, so it actually tastes of something?' Susy talks to her, but looks at me: 'No salt, Doña Mirta, you know you can't.' My grandmother dissents: 'And why do I have to swallow so many pills if afterwards I'm still going to be given food without any salt?' Susy is pragmatic: 'You'll have to talk to the doctor about that.' And she adds, turning towards me: 'You two will be finishing up soon, won't you?' I don't get to answer, my grandmother answers: 'This is the boy who passes on everything you call. We're adding these points one bean at a time!'

It's her turn to shuffle, but first I want her to tell me who this colonel was. She hesitates again, what am I talking about? The colonel you mentioned, who you wanted to talk to or who you talked to. Vilanova?, she asks me. And I don't know, I have no way of knowing, but I tell her yeah, I tell her I suppose so. Vilanova, yes. Vilanova.

Vilanova, my grandmother explains, was an old friend of your grandfather Anselmo's. They met on one of those trips your grandfather used to make, every once in a while, to Buenos Aires, on business. You could tell they got along famously and they began to exchange confidences. He talked to me about that man, he thought highly of him. After some time we went to live in Buenos Aires (we went, my grandmother says, not we came, I've no idea why) and there the two of them started to have dealings more often. Until, as happens in such cases, us wives ended up meeting too, on some visit we paid to their house, or they paid to ours. I liked his wife, a nice woman, very proper; only I can't seem to remember her name.

I tell her it doesn't matter, to go on with the thing about the colonel. But she doesn't like having forgotten, or having noticed that she's forgotten. She forces herself at the memory, but can't get there. How's it possible?, she objects. And we were such friends! Because we did become friends too, quite apart from our husbands. And we chatted for ages on the telephone, sharing the things in our lives, as well as visiting each other all the time, with your grandfather and with the colonel. Nelly? Was her name Nelly? I think she was called Nelly. Or rather, Nélida; and then she'd go by Nelly. Could that be it? Does that sound right?

I say yes: I think that sounds right. That way she won't torment herself any more and that way she'll tell me once and for all if she did or didn't talk to this Colonel Vilanova.

'Are you dealing or is it me?' she says and points to the cards.

'You,' I say.

But first I ask her to tell me.

'Tell you what?,' she says.

If you did speak to this Colonel Vilanova or not.

I did speak to him. Yes, I called him and spoke to him.

The assistant approaches again. She is now wearing a maroon overall. She tells us, or reminds us, that dinner is to be served soon. 'That's right,' replies my grandmother, 'I can smell it already.' And then she asks: 'What do we have today?' 'Chicken and mash,' says the assistant, as though for the first time. My grandmother approves, but remarks: 'I hope they put some salt on it.' The assistant, neutrally: 'Can't be with salt, Doña Mirta. Your doctor said.' My grandmother is annoyed: 'In that case you might as well serve me the sole of a tennis shoe, it would taste the same.' The assistant doesn't reply, she smiles dutifully, and leaves.

You were telling me, I say, grandma, that you talked to Colonel Vilanova.

She looks at me.

I did, yes. I called him on the telephone. I telephoned his house. If his wife had answered, I was going to ask her to put him on. But there was no need. He answered.

And, I ask, what did you say to him?

My grandmother picks the cards up off the table, straightens them out, starts to shuffle.

I told him, she says, that I was very worried: extremely worried. Why? Because of my son's friendships. Which son? Angelito, the eldest. I told him he was a good lad, conscientious, responsible. But that he was a very generous lad too, so that those other reprobates were taking advantage and using him for their communications. I told him about the strange names, I told him what I suspected.

My grandmother places the deck of cards sharply down on the table for me to cut. But I don't cut. I look at her.

And he didn't say, oh no, not like your grandfather, he didn't say I was delirious, I'd been watching too many movies. What I'd said he thought was actually very sensible, they were things people were talking about in the newspapers. It was just, your grandfather was very naïve, you know that, so naïve. And then his heart didn't hold out. That's how good he was.

My grandmother gestures towards the pack, for me to cut. But I don't cut. I look at her.

And what did he say to you?, I say. He said I might be on the right track, says my grandmother: that this was no fantasy. But there was nothing he could do about something so general. He couldn't notify anyone, he wasn't going to give anyone a warning without having more details. Then, says my grandmother, I thanked him, I sent my best to his wife, asked him please not to mention anything to Anselmo, and said goodbye. And from then on, she says, I tried to eavesdrop a bit more. That was all, she says: just eavesdropping a bit more.

She broods a while, shaking her head a little, seeming to mutter to herself.

I was so afraid they were getting your father mixed up in something, she explains.

She gestures towards the pack again. I do nothing, and she goes on.

Until one fine day, when I was listening in, she says, I heard they were arranging a meeting in Castelar. Your father, again, had come to the house, we'd drunk mate in the kitchen for a bit, then he asked if he could borrow the phone. I listened in, says my grandmother: they were arranging a meeting in Castelar. On such-and-such a day and at such-and-such a time. He named Emilio several times, Emilio this, Emilio that, Emilio's house. But it was the first time in my life I'd ever heard him mention that name. I deduced that he was passing on some code. Your grandfather told me I was making it up, but Colonel Vilanova said no I wasn't, that I was right, that this was how those people did things, that it was just like the newspapers described. Who could this so-called Emilio be? I knew, says my grandmother, that Luisito was the one who lived in Castelar. Honestly, she says to me, so many little stories about him, how could I not know where he lived, which his house was. I was very sorry to discover that Luisito was already mixed up in the business too. Ah, yes, so very sorry. But mostly I was scared about how they were involving your father. Because I was fond of Luisito, of course. Honestly, I'd known him since he was just a little kid. But a son is a son. And what most scared me was them dragging your father in too.

My grandmother sighs, looks around her: the more or less helpless old ladies she lives with now, the staff laying the long table in the middle, the blue rectangle of a window getting gradually darker as night draws in. She also looks at her own hands, the palms first and then the backs, she looks at the small table on which we're playing today's game of truco, she looks at the waiting deck, held out for cutting (but she doesn't insist, she doesn't remember). The radio keeps on playing, so bland and so blending-in that it's become easy not to hear it. On the TV, the end of the horseraces at the Palermo hippodrome (sand track) and the San Isidro hippodrome (turf track).

About Luisito, continues my grandmother, I knew, yes, I knew he lived in Castelar, a block from the station, right opposite the Gigante supermarket (he just needed to cross the street whenever they needed something); I knew the house had a kind of little garden in the front, with a plaster Pinocchio in the middle (they gave Luisito a really hard time because of his plaster Pinocchio, there was even a period when they nicknamed him Pinocchio, then I think the joke passed). I'd also learned he'd recently bought himself a used Peugeot 504, a bit battered but working, because they were all just crazy about the sunroof (it seems Luisito's girlfriend liked riding at full speed with half her body out of it).

Then I, says my grandmother, called Colonel Vilanova. I called him and he answered and I said: 'Colonel, this is Mirta, Mirta López, Anselmo Saldaña's wife.' And he told me Nelly wasn't home just then (ah yes, she was called Nelly), that she'd gone out to do some errand or other. And I said to him: 'It doesn't matter that she's out, colonel, as I'm calling to speak to you.' And I talked to him about the little house in Castelar, I talked to him about the little garden out front, I talked to him about the plaster Pinocchio. I said to him: right opposite the Gigante, a block from the station. I mentioned the Peugeot 504, the one with the sunroof. And finally I said to him: on such-and-such a day at such-and-such a time. A meeting.

My grandmother looks at the deck of cards.

'Whose turn is it to deal?' she says.

'Yours,' I say.

She starts to shuffle. She doesn't remember that she's done it already. Her shuffling is light, airy, weightless, almost immaterial. Just a little faster and the cards wouldn't have been visible at all. Finally she sets the deck down firmly on the table, for me to cut.

But I don't cut.

What did the colonel say to you?, I say instead.

What did he say to me?, says my grandmother. He said thank you, that having these solid clues he was going to look into some things himself; he said this initiative of mine was doing my son a big favour, but it was doing the country a favour too. A big favour to my son, he said, getting him away from these wicked friendships, but also a big favour to the country. And that we had to take care of Argentina, all of us together.

My grandmother tears up a little.

I understand, and she knows it.

When that day came, she says, I felt a sort of remorse. I was fond of Luisito, I'd known him since he was just a kid. I thought: Better to get arrested and have to put up with prison than having twenty bullets in his body. Because back then people were getting killed every day. But it did give me a kind of remorse. Or a hunch, a foreboding, something like that, says my grandmother. So I picked up the telephone and called your father's apartment. I wanted to invite him to come over to drink a few mates, to chat about nothing at all. It was your mother who answered. I thought she sounded tired. She said: 'Ángel's gone out.' I said 'Why don't you both come round here for some mates?' She said: 'The thing is, Ángel's not here. He's gone out.' I said: 'When he's back, then.' She said: 'He's back late.' I said: 'Where's he gone?' She hesitated, it felt to me like she hesitated. 'He's gone out with his friends,' she said. I got scared: 'But just around the neighbourhood.' 'Oh no, no,' she said, 'Somewhere out in Greater Buenos Aires.' Then my heart skipped a beat, and as it did I exclaimed 'Castelar?' Susana was surprised. Hard to say on the phone, but I thought she got chilly. 'How do you know?' she said. 'He told me,' I said. She didn't believe me, but she didn't suspect anything either. 'I'd best let you get on, then,' I said. She said to me: 'See you, Mirta, hi to Anselmo.'

My grandmother is crying. I watch her crying.

I cut off the call, she says, and I got desperate, I phoned the colonel's house. It rang and rang and rang, but nobody picked up. I thought that maybe, in my

149

nervousness, I'd dialled wrong. I called again. It rang and rang. There was nobody there. I forced myself to think that there was no way Ángel was going to take part in any meeting that was reprehensible. He must have gone someplace else. Or that the meeting at Luisito's, over in Castelar, had nothing to do with all the terrible things happening in the country in those years. And that I was going to have to apologise, for sticking my nose in, to good Colonel Vilanova. Or, if it came to it, that Ángel could clarify his situation and the business wouldn't have to get out of hand. I told myself all this, says my grand-mother, to calm myself down; but my desperation went on. It went on, and more than that, it grew. What was I to do?, says my grandmother.

What did you do?, I say.

She clasps her hands. Are they shaking? They don't look like the same hands that just a moment ago were shuffling the cards and tossing them into the game.

I called your uncle, my grandmother said. Who else could I turn to?

Roberto, I specify.

Yes, Roberto, she says. He didn't have children yet. Cristina did, she already had Dieguito, still just a baby. But also Roberto had a car. A Fiat, one of those little round ones. A Fiat 600, I specify. She shrugs: I suppose so. I told him what was going on. I didn't tell him everything, why would I? I didn't give him details, there was no need. I told him as much as necessary. Besides we needed to act as fast as we could. Why waste time explaining? I told him what was necessary and no more. I changed things a little, turned them around a little: I said, Rober, a friend of your brother's has just told me the house is going to fall down. That bit of the story I changed, as it wasn't the most important thing. Most important was going to Luisito's as soon as possible and getting Angelito out of there. I think Roberto had been to the house before, as a boy, he'd gone with your father, as he knew Luisito too; anyway I gave him all the information he needed: the station, the block, the Gigante supermarket, the little front garden, the plaster Pinocchio, the Peugeot 504, the sunroof.

My grandmother brings her hands together, as if to pray: if only he'd had a telephone! But no, he didn't. Luisito was the one who usually made contact, he'd take advantage of being at work to call from there, he was in an office. But not at home, no, he didn't have a telephone. In those days, says my grandmother, it wasn't so easy getting a telephone at home; for a start, it was very expensive, and even so, even if you had the money, you'd go onto a waiting list and it could take them more than a year to install it. And that was here in the city. Out in Greater Buenos Aires, it doesn't even bear thinking about. So in Luisito's house there was no phone, so he couldn't be called, he'd have to go over there.

And Roberto went, I say. Roberto went, yes, she says.

An assistant walks past and looks at us: she isn't the first one who'd approached us, nor is it Susy, the second; it's another, and at some distance she reprimands her: 'Don't get yourself worked up, Doña Mirta, you'll set off your blood pressure.' The same technique: the line is really directed at me, not to get my grandmother going, not to let her get agitated. But she answers, raising her voice: 'Ah, that's just what I need, dearie. Now I'm not even allowed to talk!' The girl walks off, murmuring: 'It's for your own good, you know.' My grandmother does not give way: 'I'm going to die, that much is true, but it'll be utter displeasure that kills me if they don't put any salt on that chicken.'

She looks at me and snorts. All the food tastes the same, she says; it tastes of nothing, she concludes, like that

Palito Ortega song. She hesitates. It is Palito Ortega, isn't it?, she wants to be sure. Yeah, that's right, Palito Ortega, I confirm it. Well, well, she says.

She takes up the thread again without my prompting.

Fortunately, Roberto understood it all in a second, she says. Maybe he knew something already? I don't know. He understood everything and he said to me: I'm on my way. He hung up without saying goodbye, that's the hurry he was in. And the thing was, he understood everything in a second and knew he had to rush. There was no other way of notifying him. And we had to get Ángel out of that house, out of that meeting, out of whatever. If there was nothing shady, so much the better. Just an awkward moment for Roberto, an apology to the colonel, and case closed. But if they had got him into some shady business, what then? If they'd tangled him up and dragged him into some shady business, what then? We had to get him out of there.

Roberto said later he didn't understand how come the little Fitito's engine didn't melt. He said he took it at more than a hundred and twenty, that the Fitito was squealing like an animal being sacrificed. He didn't run red lights, he said, so he wouldn't get stopped by the police, but he stepped hard on the gas all the way down Gaona: he went past the medical centre, past the Hospital Israelita, joined Juan B. Justo, past the Vélez pitch (it was almost ready, the football World Cup was coming), across General Paz and then headed for the suburbs.

Suddenly my grandmother seems to understand, or to remember, who she's talking to exactly. But you know this story already, she says. This part, yes, I say. Not the other part. Ah, no, no, of course, she smiles, not the other part.

Sweating and scared to death, my uncle arrived at Castelar. Now he needed to get across the tracks and he found the barrier lowered. The train was at the station, it was the one heading in towards the capital. He had to wait for people to get off. He had to wait for the guard to glance down the platform to blow the whistle. He had to wait for the train finally to start up and pull away, carriage by carriage, on the other side of the barrier. And he had to wait for it to get some distance away, a hundred or two hundred metres; because until it was some distance away, the barrier guard in his little wooden hut, as a precaution, wasn't going to activate the mechanism to raise the barrier and let people through.

Until finally it rose and people were let through, and Roberto sped ahead, punishing the Fitito's shock-absorbers with his haste, and they were already pretty worn out even before that. He went on, turned the corner and was about to go the last block before reaching Luis's house. But he couldn't do it, or he didn't need to; because no sooner had he turned the corner than he met a barrier made up of police squad cars and army vans. Cutting off the street, waking the neighbourhood, surrounding Luis's house. Luis's house that was now empty, that had already been emptied out.

Roberto left the car at the side of the road, got out and mingled with the onlookers. Because all this was just the threshold, the threshold and access door, to the kingdom of the clandestine, to the hell of what isn't known and can never be known. But at the same time it was happening in full view of everybody. Concealed and shown, both at the same time, simultaneously secret and visible, at once ordered and illegal. When shots rang out (because yes: shots did ring out), people retreated into their houses, lowered their blinds, shut their eyes, bowed their heads, withdrew. No sooner had the noise subsided, though, than the neighbours around the place leaned out again, they eyed and they pried, they stepped out into their doorways, even congregating on the pavement. They wanted to see, and they saw.

Roberto arrived at the time of versions and rumours. It was said that there'd been a brief exchange of gunfire, or some gunfire without any exchange. That a subversive cell had fallen, which had been hidden in a house in the neighbourhood. Soldiers came first, and then the provincial police. It was said that there was no one left in the house now. That there'd been seven or eight subversives hidden inside there, that they'd all been taken out. Two of them bloody, apparently dead. The others detained. It was said that among the group there was also a woman. Where did they take her? Impossible to know that. Go ask at the police station? There was nothing to prevent him doing that, but they would have laughed in his face. Going inside the house, was that a possibility? Gestures of disbelief. Who would be so stupid as to want to go into the house in a situation like this? The cops would have left a couple of agents stationed on the door. To prevent anyone from stealing? More incredulity, and also a sinister laugh. To prevent? Prevent? So that they could go in and do the plundering themselves as soon as it got dark.

On another part of the pavement, two women who lived around there were discussing whether it was true that the subversives were putting bombs in kindergartens or if this was a lie that the government itself had started. Someone confirmed it, yes, that was just it: there'd been two people killed, he'd seen them with his own eyes. That they'd brought them out without covering them up or anything, laid out on a board. That the others were shoved out and beaten out, that they were loaded onto two blue vans, unmarked, and taken away, wheels screeching, but without putting on sirens or anything. Roberto didn't want to pry any more. He wandered and listened a little longer to people's comments, then he turned around and left.

My grandmother says that, not having heard anything, she contacted Colonel Vilanova once again. She had to call several times to do this, it wasn't easy to get hold of him; sometimes the phone rang and rang, without anyone answering; other times, it was Nelly, her friend, who picked up, and she, doubtful, didn't cut off the call by slamming the handset down abruptly, but pressing her fingers gently on the cradle.

When at last she managed to find him, she laid out all her anguish. They didn't know anything about Ángel: if he'd been killed that day (since there had been, people said, two killed) or if he'd been detained; and if he was detained, then where, and in what state. My grandmother remained convinced, she says, that if they allowed him to give his relevant deposition, Ángel would undoubtedly be able to clarify things. The colonel promised to carry out his inquiries.

But nothing ever came from him, he never contributed or remedied anything. In fact, they didn't see him again until the night of my grandfather's wake, at Zucotti's, on Avenida Córdoba. That same day the football World Cup had started. Ah, how poor Anselmo suffered, says my grandmother. Until his heart said enough was enough. He died at half-time of the opening game. They held their wake for him that night: Zucotti's, Avenida Córdoba. After midnight, the colonel showed up. Nelly, his wife, was with him. He gave his sincere condolences, exchanged hugs and pats on the back. As soon as they could, they approached him: first Roberto and my grandmother, and later my aunt Cristina too. He gave all of them the same answer: that he was working his contacts, but nobody knew anything. That they could count on him to help, and all the more after this tragedy with Anselmo, but that he couldn't do any more than this, that nobody knew anything.

My grandmother takes the pack of cards from the table and starts to shuffle again. It's the third time, but she doesn't notice. She shuffles and shuffles. I ask her at what moment she had revealed, to Uncle Roberto specifically, or to the family in general, that the warning call, that time, hadn't been made by Colonel Vilanova to her, but the opposite, that she had made it to Colonel Vilanova. My grandmother smiles. She is crying silently, her face still and tears streaming. And at the same time she smiles.

She shuffles for several minutes. She shuffles too much.

Finally she sets down the deck of cards, she leaves it there for me to cut.

I don't move, I keep looking at her.

'You're just killing time so the game won't end,' she says. 'You're scared of losing.'

With her fingertips she pushes the deck of cards a little closer towards me. She is pushing it nearer, so that I'll cut.

I don't move, I keep looking at her.

Until, at last, I make up my mind and I cut.

Then she resolutely places one half on top of the other and deals at great speed.

I receive my three cards, fan them out.

My grandmother does the same.

My hand is a seven of swords, a five of swords, a twelve of clubs.

'Envido,' I say.

'I'm in,' she says.

'Thirty-two,' I say.

She grumbles.

'It's yours,' she says.

I think for a moment then decide to play the twelve.

I hope I'll get away with it. I do. My grandmother plays just a seven of cups. I try to force her hand, and without calling, I play the five of swords, expressionless, nothing emphatic. But my grandmother gets the whole thing.

'Ah, cunning little swine,' she says.

And she throws in the towel.

I show her the envido, and note down the points. It's three to me. There's three points separating my grandmother and me and I'm three away from winning the game. Realising this makes me anxious. She, on the other hand, looks calm.

I shuffle, she cuts, I deal.

My grandmother fans out her three cards extremely slowly. And she opens them only as much as is necessary, no more than necessary, to see the hand she's been dealt.

She plays a three of swords.

'Envido,' I say.

I've got nothing. Absolutely nothing at all. Will she realise?

'I'll pass,' she says.

She hasn't realised. Or she hasn't got anything either. Nothing at all.

My hand: a seven of cups, a four of coins, the seven of swords.

I decide to let her have the first round, though there are orthodoxies to recommend the contrary. I play the four of coins.

She nods, beats that one and then plays low. A six of cups. A perfect fit, as I expected. I beat it with the seven of cups. I get excited.

'Truco!' I say.

I sound defiant.

'I'm in,' she says.

She sounds indifferent.

With a gesture of refutation, although there's nothing

I'm refuting, I conclude with my seven of swords.

'Ah, little swine,' she says.

But she looks at me. And she smiles.

'Retruco,' she says.

I stare hard at her, my eyebrows raised. She just smiles. She's got one card left in her hand. I've already played my three.

Is she lying? Pressuring me? Trying to force my hand?

I look at her and she looks at me. I'm searching for some gesture, however tiny, a suggestion, any clue. I don't find it.

I try to reason out the situation. Let her say, if she wants to, that I play truco like it was chess. I try to reason it out.

We're at twenty-eight to twenty-four. If I win the truco, which I've already called and she's already said she's in, I gain two points and win the game. So she, then, has no choice. She's doubling the bet to scare me. It's her last resort, giving the impression of solvency to make me back down; because if she doesn't do that, I've already got the game won.

But if that's the case, maybe she should blink, clear her throat, swallow. And she doesn't.

Nor does she look confident. Or nervous about my response. She just looks at me. And smiles.

'I said *retruco*,' she says.

I nod.

'I'm in,' I say.

She throws down the ace of clubs, hard, with an emphatic laugh.

'Ah, and the kid's screwed up!' she exclaims.

I gather up the cards purely out of annoyance, to remove what's happened from my sight, because it's my grandmother whose turn it is to shuffle.

I make a note on the piece of paper. One stroke for

me. Three for her. I've got one point on her now.

She shuffles. I cut. She deals. Her smile continues, meanwhile. It leaves her when she sees the hand that's come to her in this round, and which she got for herself. Or that's the impression she's giving me, I don't know.

I've got two elevens (swords and coins), and a two (cups). For the envido, nothing. Nothing. I can't risk it. I don't. Wordlessly, I play the two.

She hesitates. But she doesn't call envido.

She checks her cards. Then she plays another two, the two of clubs. She positions it, meticulously, on top of mine.

I'm left with two weak cards. I play without speaking. Whichever of the two elevens I play, it makes no difference. I choose to play the eleven of swords, as if that mattered, as if that changed anything. Feels more aggressive. Makes me feel safer.

'Truco,' says my grandmother.

'I'll pass,' I say.

I didn't even need to think. It would have been crazy to risk it.

'Ah, what a baby!' she says. 'So you haven't got over your little scare, then?'

She brings her cards to the deck, without letting me see them, and pushes the deck over for me to shuffle.

'How are we doing?'

'Both on twenty-eight,' I say.

She makes a sign of agreement, I don't know what it means.

Cautiously, one of the assistants approaches. My grandmother preempts her: 'We're just finishing, dear. Just one hand left.' Still the woman wants to explain: 'We're serving in five minutes.' My grandmother acknowledges this: 'I know, I know, I can smell it. You can chuck the salt on now, we're on our last hand and I'll be there.'

I shuffle the cards, I shuffle and shuffle.

I give them to her to cut, she cuts. I deal.

The cards travel one by one and don't quite come together on that side of the table, right in front of her hands. Mine, though, which I drop close to me, fall one on top of the other.

We take our time to arrange, to peer at them, to evaluate.

I've got a two of swords, a twelve of coins and the ace of clubs.

Nothing for the envido, but for a truco I'm in a more than strong position.

Envido, in any case, she does not call. She plays a three directly. The three of coins.

I let it go by with the twelve of coins, once again disregarding the conventional slogans. The twelve and the three: the table is suddenly filled with gold coins, with sparkling, with yellow, with brilliance.

My grandmother stops to think. Will she call or won't she? She doesn't. In silence she plays a one of cups. I tell myself: she's got nothing. She just leaves it there, quite still, on the table, on the gold coins. I tell myself: she's got nothing left. I look at her and she looks at me. I tell myself: she's got nothing left.

I beat her one of cups with the two of swords.

And I take a pause, to evaluate, carefully, what it would be best for me to do. But the pause is false and the evaluation is false and the carefulness is false. I've got the ace of clubs in my hand, I've got the game almost won. She would need, then, to have the ace of swords, and I don't think she does. But if I'm too quick to call, if I come across as too cocky, she could get suspicious, she could say 'I'll pass' and that'd be that; I'd get only one point and there'd still be all to play for. So I falsely fabricate my cautiousness, I construct my hesitancy for her. I take my time, scratch my chin. Turns out looking uncertain isn't at all hard for me. She waits, expressionless.

'Truco,' I say.

'I'm in,' she says.

I managed to sound meek, even timid. But she answered me immediately, one might almost say automatically, as if to suggest that her acceptance had already been decided.

We look at each other. Everything has been said. Now it's just a matter of showing our cards and the game will be over.

I nod and I smile and play my ace of clubs.

She sees it and raises her eyebrows. Is she surprised? I don't know.

She looks at her card, she looks at me.

It's the last card of the game. The last one she'll play. She raises it gently, perhaps to throw it onto the table and win, perhaps to drop it onto the deck and surrender.

Meanwhile, of course, she looks at me and smiles.

APPENDIX: How to Play Truco

Truco is a trick-taking card game using a Spanish deck, which is associated with gaucho culture (writers like José Hernández and Borges have devoted some famous pages to it), and very popular in Argentina, Uruguay, Paraguay, Chile and some parts of Brazil. It can be played with two, three, four or six players. For each hand, each player is dealt three cards, which are unseen by their opponents; the aim of the game is to win as many hands as possible, so as to be the first to reach thirty points.

The Spanish deck used in truco consists of forty cards. They are divided into four suits (swords, clubs, cups and coins), with a scale of values, from highest to lowest, as follows:

Ace of swords
Ace of clubs
Seven of swords ('siete bravo')
Seven of coins
All the threes
All the twos
Aces of coins and cups ('false aces')

All the twelves (kings)
All the elevens (knights)
All the tens (knaves)
Sevens of clubs and cups
All the sixes
All the fives
All the fours.

There are two ways of winning points in truco: with an envido (if you hold two cards of the same suit), or truco (winning tricks as the cards are played in turn, as determined by the scale of values of the cards, above).

Note that there is also an optional variation to the game, involving a third way of winning points, called flor. Playing flor cancels out an envido, and it must be called when a player (or a member of a playing pair) receives three cards of the same suit. Often it is not made explicit in advance whether a game is being played 'with flor' (the likelihood of one happening is low, around 4.8%), which can lead to heated discussion over the course of a game (usually when a player discovers a flor in his hand) as to whether or not this method of winning points had been agreed.

Language has a performative function during the game, since the mere fact of speaking a play (calling 'envido' or calling 'truco', say) implies playing it. Faced with such a call, the opponent has three options: say 'quiero' (I'm in) and play their hand; say 'no quiero' (pass) and lose their points; or raise the bet (there are several possible phrases for doing this, including responding to a 'truco' with a 'retruco'), which then means waiting for their opponent to respond. If an envido is refused, the player loses their points; if a truco is refused, points are lost and the hand is ended. Since speaking the play implies playing it, if a player wants to refer in conversation to a play without committing themselves, they need to use a complex slang of equivalent terms, to avoid inadvertently making the play concrete.

The game depends substantially on an ability to lie, and to speculate whether an opponent is lying or telling the truth. One of the essential gifts of a good player is to make their opponent believe they have a good hand when their cards are actually bad and vice versa. So when the game is at its most critical moments, truco can turn into a psychological duel of gestures, intrigues, deceptions and suspicions.

Michel Nieva

Director & Editor: Carolina Orloff
Director: Samuel McDowell

www.charcopress.com

Confession was published on
80gsm Munken Premium Cream paper.

The text was designed using Bembo 11.5 and ITC Galliard.

Printed in June 2023 by TJ Books
Padstow, Cornwall, PL28 8RW using responsibly
sourced paper and environmentally-friendly adhesive.